IN SEARCH
OF
THE FERN FLOWER

by

TERESA PALICZKA

To Rita

from

Teresa Paliczka

2/12/2016

RB
Rossendale Books

Published by Lulu Enterprises Inc.
3101 Hillsborough Street
Suite 210
Raleigh, NC 27607-5436
United States of America

Published in paperback 2015
Category: Fiction
Copyright Teresa Paliczka © 2015
ISBN : 978-1-326-26295-2

All rights reserved, Copyright under Berne Copyright Convention and Pan American Convention. No part of this book may be reproduced, stored in a retrieval system, or transmitted in any form or by any means, electronic, mechanical, photocopying, recording or otherwise, without prior permission of the author. The author's moral rights have been asserted.

This is a work of fiction. Names, characters, corporations, institutions, organisations, events or locales in this novel are either the product of the author's imagination or, if real, used fictitiously. Any resemblance to actual persons (living or dead) is entirely coincidental.

Dedication

To those who suffer,
To those who feel the sufferings of others and ask:
"WHY?"

CONTENTS

INTRODUCTION 7
Chapter 1   THE SEARCH 9
Chapter 2   IS THIS ALL AN IMAGINATION? 21
Chapter 3   THE BLACK KITTEN 26
Chapter 4   MORE QUESTIONS 32
Chapter 5   DREAMS AND REALITIES 40
Chapter 6   LEO'S PAINTING 50
Chapter 7   THE SEVENTH HEAVEN 57
Chapter 8   OLIVER 63
Chapter 9   KOTECK 68
Chapter 10 SNOWFLAKE 77
Chapter 11 A BROKEN BRIDGE 82
Chapter 12 SYLVIA'S MEMORIES 94
Chapter 13 THE FOOTPRINTS 105
Chapter 14 FERN FLOWERS ARE SHY 115

INTRODUCTION

Some ancient legends and myths survive - or, at least their echoes can still be heard in the collective memories of human race, poems and songs for many centuries, throughout turbulent events of history, changing cultures and beliefs. One of them comes from the pre-Christian era in Poland, when pagan gods, goddesses, fairies and miracle making deities used to dwell in the depths of wild forests: the legend of the fern flower that blooms at midnight at the time of the summer solstice on the 21st of June - but only those who have pure hearts can see its splendid and unearthly beauty.

This book is a collection of fictional and correlative stories about people from different places and times whose lives seem to reflect some of the radiance of "pure hearts" - whether they have ever scanned the ferns with their torches at the time of the summer solstice, or not - and about people of another kind, with little or no interest in the qualities of their hearts.

It also includes the stories about other sentient beings on our earth: the animals for whom the contacts with various people brought either joys or sufferings. And this evokes the timeless, unfathomable Big Question: "Why do the innocents have to suffer?"

As some life events of both humans and animals seem to be woven together in a mysterious way, even when separated by time and space, yet other Big Questions emerge: "Is there a life after the physical death?". "Is the concept of reincarnation realistic or absurd?"

No clear-cut, undeniable Answers. Seeking for Truth, we are like children in a dark forest, with their little torches trying to find the elusive fern flower.

Yet... if we abandon the search we remain trapped in the even darker and meaningless jungle of our dark hearts, where no flowers of any kind ever grow...

Chapter 1

THE SEARCH

Walk at night into depths of the forest
Where ferns dream in the sleepy moonlight,
Stop and look all around you in silence,
With your heart's eyes wide open, alive
:

Only silvery shimmers on dark leaves,
Only owl's hooting cries far away,
Only...when thoughts are still, heart grows wiser:
Something glows in the ferns...like a ray
:

That had fallen from skies. With the beauty
Of a thousand bright rainbows and stars
Blooms in woods. And those know who have seen it
:

Ferns do flower when watched with pure hearts!

We all loved this song. Jim, our most popular singer and composer at the time, knew how - with his deep, soul-stirring baritone - make us feel as though we were transported from the solid reality of our living room where we sat, into the world of his magic. Even after the record player had stopped.

Angela, my five year old sister was the first one

to break the silence.

"Julia," - she asked me (because I was ten years older than her, she simply assumed that I always have ready answers to all her questions) - "why I had never seen the fern flower?"

I paused, realising how pitiably limited my reserve of "ready answers" was and tried to postpone my reply. "Angela," - I said - "but are you sure you have the pure heart?"

Angela suddenly looked sad. "I don't know..." - she whispered.

I felt guilty. How a five year old could guess that I was only joking? At that age they take in all so literally!

Barbara, my best friend came to rescue. "Angela,"- she said - "you have the purest heart one could ever have!"

Angela cheered up, but was not quite satisfied. "How do you know that?" - she inquired.

"Because you are too young to do anything really bad." Barbara replied.

"You mean... like being very naughty?"

This time it was my turn. "It is more than being naughty." - I said - "It is like... when Karl was beating Lacy in his garden... do you remember?"

Yes, she remembered as well as I did.

* * * * *

It happened two years ago. Angela and I were walking along our street, passing Karl's house, when we heard those plaintive whinings. We stopped.

In his front garden Karl was holding a small yellow dog by the scruff of his neck, with the clenched fist of another hand punching hard the screaming, wriggling desperately little creature. We had to intervene.

"Stop it!" -I shouted.

Karl looked at me, his eyes glaring: "She steals the food from the kitchen. She needs the lesson!"

"But she is only a puppy..." I started but did not finished. As Karl now turned his rage at us, for a moment he lost his hold on the pup who slipped out of his grasp and ran through the half-open gate straight towards us. I grabbed her in my arms and backed away from the house. Angela was crying, clinging to me.

"You can take her if you want!" - shouted Karl - "I don't want the bastard!"

We walked home, the puppy in my arms quiet now, only still panting.

Angela made for her a little nest with the pillows on her bed, then we had to subject our faces and hands to the storm of the puppy's exhilarated, wet kisses. We named her Lacy. She was now our dog... or, strictly speaking, Angela's dog, her love and companion, her inseparable shadow.

Our parents accepted Lacy and all that came with her: the muddy footprints on carpets and chairs, our night sleep disturbed by her high-pitched puppyish barks (when a stray cat dared to venture too close to our window), and few other things... all in the welcome exchange for her unbounded, overflowing love for us - and equally unbounded, overflowing and sometimes very unrestrained joy of life.

Lacy grew up to become the middle-sized, cross-breed (only God knew of what parentage!), with the shiny yellow coat and the big, black, expressive eyes. Those big eyes were so quick to spot a slightest sign of our displeasure when her exuberant behaviour became "less acceptable". Then, Lacy would lie down, her eyes apologetic, her tail wagging frantically, hoping for forgiveness. She didn't like us being upset, she badly wanted to share her happiness with everyone around her! Afterwards, the particular behaviour became less and less frequent to die out in course of few weeks. "Training" Lacy was an easy task!

The only times when Lacy refused to comply with our requests, pleadings and coaxings were when we decided to pass Karl's house. There was no way to stop her screaming and pulling on leash in the opposite direction, so finally we gave in to her will.

Anyway, it didn't matter. The other way was just as short to get us to the fields. Maybe she was right after all? Who wants to revive the sad memories of the past? She wanted to forget, to erase all their traces from the history of her puppyhood. Life was so great now... why to allow any dark shadow to creep into it?

Maybe she was right...

* * * * *

Now she was dozing peacefully on the settee, her head as usual on Angela's lap. Angela was quiet, pondering over what I had said. Then she concluded: "Karl is bad because he hurt Lacy, he doesn't have the pure heart. But I am only naughty... sometimes, so I have one!" - she exclaimed.

"That's right," - I said - "Angela, you are very wise now!"

"So, I can see the fern flower, can I?"

Another hard question. Once more, Barbara came to help: "Angela...do you remember when the Father Christmas came to your house with the presents?"

"But he was only uncle Tom dressed like Father Christmas!"

"Yes." - Barbara was very patient - "Yet you liked your present?"

"Yes."

"And you liked uncle Tom disguised as Father Christmas?"

"Yes, that was very nice!" - Angela smiled.

"And," - Barbara continued - "It is also nice to read the fairy tales... like those of Cinderella and

Snow White... even when we know they are not true."

Angela thought about it for a while : "You mean that the story about the fern flower is nice but it is not true?"

"Yes,"- Barbara replied - "but does it matter? It was so nice to listen to the song about it!"

Angela was clearly disappointed, yet not quite convinced. "It would be even nicer to go to the woods and see if this is true! Julia," - now she turned to me - "Can we go?"

"Not at night!" - I cried out - "It is very dark over there!"

"We can take our torches!" - Angela was very resourceful.

"We still have two weeks to go before the twenty-first of the June,"- I was hoping that by that time she may forget all about it - "the legend says that the fern only blooms at that time, at the night of the summer solstice... do you remember? And your birthday is on the twentieth of June, one day before." - I tried to change the subject - "What you would like for your birthday present, Angela?"

My little sister's reply came instantly, with no hesitation: "I want to go to the woods on the twenty-first of June and see the fern flower! And..." - she continued - "I want also you to come with me! And you, Barbara! And Lacy too! We all have the pure hearts, we may see the flower!"

Just then, Lacy jumped off the settee and ran

to the front door, barking excitedly. She heard - few seconds before we did - the sound of our parents' car pulling into the drive. They were returning from their visit to uncle Tom.

Angela followed Lacy. As soon as the door opened she threw herself into Molly's (our mother) arms, telling her hurriedly what I and Barbara had said, what she thinks about it and why she wants this unusual present for her birthday.

More arguments, counter-arguments, persuasions and explanations followed afterward. Nothing could convince our (so young!) seeker for truth of the impracticality and even possible pitfalls of her project! In conclusion, Terry (our father) pointed out that although habits and rules are very useful and should be upheld, there are also some rare exceptions. Yes, Angela's wish is very unique, but birthdays are supposed to be the joyful events. Who would like to deny her the fulfilment of this wish at that time? We all agreed.

The plan had been drawn up: Angela, I, Barbara (subject to her parents' permission), and Terry ("just in case" for our protection, though there were no wolves in English forests at the end of the twentieth century!) and (of course!) Lacy will take the short trip to the nearby woodland at the time of the summer solstice, to see... *to see what?*

"We don't know," - I said (now becoming more and more involved in the project) - "this is a mystery. As such, it cannot be revealed, not yet.

But trying to find out may be quite a fun!"

Angela was overjoyed.

"And..." - Barbara called from the door, leaving our house - "don't forget to check your torches' batteries before we go!"

* * * * *

Starry night. Clear and peaceful. We were walking across the field towards the woods, higher up on the hill. The full moon hovered above it, almost touching the treetops. On the other side, all around the horizon, the sky was displaying its night splendour, with lavish generosity for all who wanted to see it.

Stars, thousands of stars aglow in the velvety black abyss above our heads... Stars... twinkling, sparkling, beaming their tale about the immensity of the great Universe holding millions of yet unsolved mysteries beyond our comprehension...

"How far away the stars are?" - asked Angela.

"Very far." - I said and added quickly: "No one can ever go as far as that!"

"Never?"

Terry, who walked beside us replied: "Maybe never or... who knows? Our astronauts had already walked on the surface of the Moon. But stars are many, many times further away." Luckily, he didn't have to explain the details of the interstellar distances as we now had reached the edge of the field.

Angela's interest turned to the steep path, leading up to the woods.

Lacy was the first one to run uphill. The place was familiar to her from our daytime walks; the novelty of the night trip was for her even more fascinating.

"Wait, Lacy!" - Angela called, her hands and knees on the bottom of the path.

Lacy ran back (steep slopes were no problem for her), placed a kiss on the girl's nose, and ran again up the path with one loud, urging bark.

Angela laughed, (they both understood each other language) and started to clamber uphill (she loved her independence and self-sufficiency).We followed her all the way to the top.

Here, the forest trees casted their shadows all around. The soft, pale moonlight was slipping through the boughs, the silvery droplets landing on the path, grasses, bushes and on us. An owl started hooting somewhere in the distance... just like in the song.

We were now approaching a small clearing, abounding with ferns, where Angela wanted to go (tonight she was the boss!), when a passing cloud overshadowed the moon, dimming its light. Now we needed our torches.

Suddenly, an anxious thought crept into my mind: what if (most likely!) Angela's starry-eyed expectation would meet the blankness of the harsh reality? How hard is it going to be to wipe away her tears of disappointment?

If I tell her that... once upon a time, someone had noticed the moonlight's reflection in the rain drops on the fern leaves that - for a moment - looked like a flower, felt exalted by the sight and created the legend that have survived in people memory for more then a thousand years... could this be the answer to Angela's question?

And...if not? Then I would try, once and for all, after Barbara's failed attempt to clarify the issue, but I would use a subtler analogy: I would tell my little sister that although running across the field toward the point where the bright rainbow touches the horizon could be a great joy, but expecting or hoping to grasp its light in one's hands would only bring a sad disappointment. We just have to distinguish between illusion and reality!

Yet... a doubt had crossed my mind: for how many centuries humans remained convinced with the undisputed certainty that the sun circled our earth and not the other way round? If the "reality" of their sight observation later has turned out to be the illusion... could it also be possible that what we now call "illusion" may turn out to be real?

"Stop philosophising, Julia!" - I told myself.

We now had reached our destination. Angela and Lacy were already there, at the edge of the clearing.

Angela stood still, calm and thoughtful, with her arms down, the little torch dangling from her hand, illuminating the ground around her feet and Lacy, sitting close to her. She seemed to look at something ahead, but *her eyes were closed!*

Barbara shone her torch at the ferns in front of her. They were there: the tall, bushy ferns with their long stems, with the exquisite pattern of their leaves... the leaves, *only the leaves...*

The dark cloud drifted away. The forest around us was there as it had been before: the trees, the ferns, the grasses, all bathed now in the silvery moonlight... and the owl's hooting in the distance... just like in the beginning of Jim's song.

Angela opened her eyes.

No, I didn't have to wipe away her tears, as there were none. Neither I needed to comfort her with my previously rehearsed lecture. My little sister looked quite happy on the way back home. She played with Lacy, laughed while sliding on her bottom downhill from the woods... yet, (and this was new!) not chattering with us as usual.

As soon as we had started across the field, Barbara couldn't restrain her curiosity.

"Angela," - she asked - "what did you see in the woods?"

Angela looked at her, surprised : "Don't you know?"

"No, I don't... why you've kept your eyes closed?"

Angela stopped abruptly. "Yes, those eyes," - she pointed to her face - "I closed them to see better with my heart's eyes! That's what Jim said in his song, to open your heart's eyes!" - she spelled out, and - clearly frustrated with my friend's lack of understanding - picked up a stick from the path, threw it for Lacy and ran after her toward our house.

*****

Apparently, she was *the only one* who had found the answer to her question that night.

Chapter 2

IS THIS ALL AN IMAGINATION?

At home, Molly greeted us with her freshly baked, delicious cakes. But Angela only nibbled one of them, said "Thank you for the lovely present!", waved goodbye and ran upstairs to her bedroom. She seemed to be overflowing with excitement, but - for some reason contrary to her nature - unwilling to share it with us.

"It is strange..." - Molly remarked - " she doesn't want to talk to us tonight!"

"Maybe she is too excited by what she has seen in the woods." - I said - "But no one else has noticed anything unusual there."

"You really mean *what she has imagined to see*?"

"Maybe...I just don't know..."

Molly looked uneasy: "I know that Angela is *different*. When she was two, she kept telling me about big, white birds in the garden that talked and played with her. Yes, I knew that 'visions' of this kind were quite common with some toddlers. They 'see' angelic playmates, white and winged like birds and think they are real. But Angela is five year old now, and very intelligent."

"She is." - said Terry (Terry was biology teacher

at school, but privately also interested in psychology and para-psychology) - "That's why she was able to learn quickly to keep her "visions" to herself, in order not to upset the others. So clever, our little girl! That's why she is so silent now."

No one had said anything for some time, then Terry spoke again: "I was thinking about something... how interesting they are: the various flows and twists of the evolution."

I thought he came off the subject. "Evolution?..." - I asked.

"Yes, the evolution. I was thinking about how in the course of millions of years the various species have developed their sight organs, in different degrees. For example, the bees have "better eyes" than us, as they can discern six wave frequencies of light spectrum, six colours - while we can only see three: red, yellow and blue. And other species see less, and some are colour-blind."

"But..." - interrupted Molly - "what that has to do with Angela and her imagination?"

"Maybe nothing." - replied Terry - "But this could be a useful allegory. Think of a hypothetical possibility of some humans becoming the *avant-garde* in the visual evolution who may see more colours, like bees... how could they explain to the rest of us that our flower gardens are more colourful that we can see?"

Molly became impatient: "It is me who still can't see what this has to do with Angela?"

"Let me finish, Molly. Some archeologists think - or suppose - that in some pre-historical age our distant ancestors were colour-blind before humans could see as we do now."

"So...?"

"So... let just assume - for the sake of my argument, if nothing else - that, in that immemorial past the evolution has taken a different path, favouring mental faculties that created science and technology, but was rather slow-paced in advancing human visual side. In that world people would see everything around them as we see it in the old black-and-white films.

"I don't think I would like to live in that world..." - I said - "it would be so sad not to enjoy the beauty of sunsets, rainbows and flowers."

"Yes, Julia," - Terry replied - "but people living in that world wouldn't know what they were missing, like colour-blind people in our times."

"They don't seem to be too upset about it."

"Yes, because they compensate with other faculties, as past generations would have done. They would be quite content in their lives. However, some of them, a small minority group would feel not so happy."

"Why?"

"Why? Because the evolution, so eager to create the very best of our species would notice its mistake and start speeding up the advancement of human sight organs. As those processes are slow and gradual, at first only few individuals would show the results, and those few would becomee the forerunners of the new future. But they would also find themselves isolated and lonely. Once they had discovered - as you, Julia have said - the beauty of sunsets and flowers, they would feel a need to share their new joys with their fellowmen... but, instead of the expected understanding they would find alienation.

'What?' - their teachers, friends and relatives would say - *'You can see something that no one else can? The science had proved that human eyes can distinguish the various degrees of the light's brightness, but not the frequencies of its spectrum. What you see comes from your imagination! Or...you may need psychiatric help...'*

That's why some of our likely ancestors could have become so lonely. Isolated. And rather disinclined to talk about what they saw, what they felt and what they thought."

Molly got up from her seat. "Terry," - she said - "Now I know what you are driving at: you think that Angela is also a kind of forerunner of the evolution, as she can see what the rest of us can't!"

"Yes." - Terry answered - "That's what I'm thinking...or assuming she may be."

"What sort of the evolution is that?"

"Not physical, but concerning an aspect of our mental and emotional make-up that seems to be calling out for the urgent uplift."

"What you are talking about, Terry?"

"I'm talking about the ability to comprehend - or, at least to catch few glimpses of this comprehension - of the things that usually lie beyond the scope of our senses, and even beyond the scope of our intellect. This faculty is not new: it has been well known to us for millennia, yet it still remains enigmatic to the mainstream science. I'm talking about *the spiritual aspect* of our mind."

"Oh, no!" - Molly would not listen to him any longer - "I'm going upstairs
to check on Angela!"

She came back after few minutes, more relaxed now and said: "She sleeps... maybe having sweet dreams about her fern flower. That's good... *in the dreams*!"

Chapter 3

THE BLACK KITTEN

Sunday was the day after our summer solstice trip, so we could sleep as long as we liked. But I woke up early with the sunlight kisses on my face and the birds' morning concert outside the window. The world was a great place to be... the real world that - at least sometimes - feels like a wonderful dream.

"Is Angela dreaming?" I got up and tiptoed to her bedroom. Lacy jumped off her bed, greeting me. I sat at the edge of the bed.

Angela was sleeping soundly, a soft smile on her face, till Lacy started barking at the door: her way to tell us that the day was too good to stay indoors.

"Julia !" - she exclaimed, sitting up and embracing me - "I had a dream!"

"Oh..." - I said - "a nice dream?"

"Yes, yes...a very nice dream!"

"Can you tell me?" - I inquired rather hesitatingly, but today my sister has allowed me to catch a glimpse of her very private world. In her excitement she could not hold her tongue any longer.

"I dreamed that I was with Lacy in the woods

at night, in the same place where the fern flower grows."

I held my breath. "Grows...?" - I asked.

"Yes, it grows there!"- Angela looked at me, rather disappointed, yet more complaisant now than she had been with Barbara last night. "Oh, Julia..." - she uttered sadly - "you haven't seen it?"

"No..."

"But why? You have the pure heart!" - she thought for a while, then added - "Maybe you will... some other time!"

"Yes, Angela. I would love to... I would love to see what it looks like?"

"It is very beautiful..." - she was struggling to find the words, but this seemed to be too hard (or impossible?) - "It is more beautiful than any other flower!"

"I understand." - I said - "Was your dream any different from what you had seen last night?"

"Yes, it was different."

"How?"

"It was also at night, but the fern flower was so bright that everything around us was bright, too...like in the day. And we were so happy looking at it, very happy... and then, something has changed."

"What?"

"I heard someone far away. Someone very sad, crying. Lacy heard it too, and started looking ahead and sniffing. Someone was coming towards us, crying. When it came closer I could hear it better. It was a mew... a cat was mewing..."

"And it came closer and closer to you?"

"Yes. He came with all that white snow around him."

"Snow...?"

"Yes, snow. A lot of snow, also moving to us, till it covered everything. It was like in winter. The big tree with the very low branches was there. The cat was trying to come out to us from under it, but it couldn't because the branch was covered with snow and heavy. I lifted the branch and took him in my arms. He was very weak and I thought he may die. He was a small cat, black. A black kitten."

"Like Tilly, Gill's cat?" - I asked. (Gill was her schoolmate and Angela often visited her house where she played with her black cat.)

"Oh, no!" - came the reply - "Tilly is big and has the white spot on his head, but this one was small and all black. I cuddled him, and Lacy started licking him all over. He started purring... we were so happy that he was alive!"

"Because you and Lacy made him feel warm!"

"Yes, Julia... that's what has happened. And then... all the snow around us was gone. It was summer again and it was day. And... and the fern flower was gone, too."

"Were you sad that it was gone?"

"No. We were so glad to have this kitten with us. He was happy, too. We walked back home.

Someone else was walking with us... a boy, but I didn't know him."

"And?"

"And then I woke up and saw you!"

"Angela..." - I said - "this was a lovely dream!"

"Yes. I'll always remember it!" - said Angela.

* * * * *

And she did. Even four years later, when she was nine, (by that time she had been moved to the higher grade in her school, as her intelligence was far ahead of her age group) the children in her class have been given a task to write an essay on any subject, real or imaginary, for their homework.

This is what Angela has written:

THE BLACK KITTEN

That night snow fell heavily in this part of the eastern Europe. And frost. Frost turned lakes into ice-skating rinks, droplets of melting snow into silvery, long icicles, hanging from roofs' edges. People snuggled around their stoves indoors, wild animals in forests under the low bushes' boughs. Hardly anyone ventured across the vast, snow-covered, frozen field, especially at night.

No footprints there... except for the narrow, single path, stretching from an isolated smallholding towards a village about a half mile away.... a small path, made by a small kitten's paws.

At the farmhouse where the kitten lived, all doors were

shut tight. Inside people were talking loudly. No one has heard his plaintive mews.

He knew there were other houses at the far end of the field, - he had been there before the snow storm - the warm, very warm houses and people who smiled and petted him. He decided to go there... across the vast, frozen field.

But he was cold and ill and had a diarrhea. Now and then he collapsed and got up again. Once he rested under the big branch of a tree that grew at the field's edge. He was exhausted and felt sleepy. But the frost was biting his paws. He dragged himself back into the field, one thought, one desire only in his mind: to the house... to the house, to the warmth!

The village was not far away now. He crawled, inching along, closer and closer till he has reached the nearest house, where he heard human voices and felt the warmth behind the front door. He sat by this door and mewed.

Someone has opened the door slightly, then shut it. The kitten mewed louder, again and again... and then, he fell silent.

Two people were living in this house: a woman and her daughter, a girl of school-going age. They were arguing.

"We can't let this cat indoors!" - the woman was trying to explain - "He is filthy, all covered in his dirt! He has his owner and his house, he'll go there!"

The girl pleaded and pleaded, to no avail. The woman has locked the door and hid the key under the pillow in her bed.

At dawn, the girl - who pretended to be asleep - waited for her mother to get up and go to the kitchen to put the kettle on, then grabbed the key and opened the front door.

A small, black , furry thing was lying there on the white snow. Motionless. Stiff and cold.

The girl knelt down, gathered the lifeless body in her arms and sobbed uncontrollably. Her mother came out of the house... and now, she too, felt tears welling up in her eyes.

Too late...too late to undo the terrible mistake, to turn the back...

What the girl didn't know at the time was that the little kitten has heard her cries. Her cries of love that came too late... her cries of grief and guilt.

Grief and guilt were strange things to him, but love... he felt it with every part of his being, in the yet untouched depths of his feline soul. The love that embraced him, comforted him and unburdened him of all agonies of his short life in his physical body.

All was bliss in this new world created by Love...

* * * * *

At school Angela received the top mark for her essay.

Chapter 4

MORE QUESTIONS

In the evening we sat around the fire in our living room, sipping tea. Winter came early this year in November, with dark nights, fogs and long rainy spells.

"Angela," - Molly said - "this is a brilliant essay. You have the talent. One day you'll be a writer."

"Thanks, Mum. I would love to be. I like writing stories."

"I'll look forward to read more of them, darling."

"But..." - Angela hesitated for a while, then asked: "will you always like what I'll write?"

"I'll always *love* what you'll write! Even... even if sometimes I may not agree with what you may express in your stories."

"Can you tell me what?"

"Yes. In your essay you have described so well and so movingly the feelings of the little kitten, abandoned on the cold night. This will help the campaign against cruelty to animals. Many people need to know that other creatures suffer, too. Only... I just don't share your belief that animals - or even us, humans have something what's called 'souls'."

"Yet, Molly..." - interrupted Terry, half-jokingly - "you like going to church for the Christmas midnight mass?"

"Of course. The lights, the music, the songs... the whole atmosphere there is lovely, especially at Christmas. It is a welcome relief from daily stresses, just as good music, poetry and all kinds of uplifting fantasies are!"

"As long as you know that they are no more than fantasies?"

"Yes, Terry. At the end of the day we have to return to our *real* lives, with all their ups and downs."

"But, Mum..." - I broke in - "what kind of relief or even hope can be in this world for all those, animals or humans, who are trapped in grim circumstances like the kitten in Angela's story... abandoned by people, by fate, or by God?"

"I don't know." - replied Molly, and then added sadly: "Life is not always based on justice. Maybe that's why we had to invent the concept of the afterlife, better and kinder, compensating for all sufferings in this life."

It was late. We were too tired to continue our debate. Lacy was already asleep, barking softly in her dream.

The rain was lashing and splashing on the windows outside.

* * * * *

Alone in my bedroom that night, many thoughts have crept into my mind and kept buzzing there like stubborn flies, driving my sleep away.

More thoughts, more questions.

Molly had no answer for me when I asked her. Angela had, by drawing it from her rich inner world of visions and dreams... for the Hope, so much sought after by all tormented beings walking through our "valley of tears"... and for some peace of mind, needed by those who are compassionate but feel powerless in the face of the immensity of their task: to wipe away *all* tears from the tear-soaked valley...

Unlike Angela, I had no access to this world of the hidden wisdom. I had never seen a flowering fern. I had never played with angelic beings in my infancy.

I was left alone with my question: "*Why* do innocents have to suffer?"

Does God, or gods, or any unknown power that had brought this world into existence has any plan or goal for its creation, other than being the source of amusement for an intelligent but heartless creator?

Any speck of kindness that already exists in most (if not all) humans?

Are we all at the mercy of the blind forces of nature which have no mercy at all?

Few years ago, Terry spoke of the evolution as being wise and purposeful, aiming to achieve the best results for living species. What is "the best"? Asked this question, most of us would reply: "It is what fulfils my needs, what makes me happy." The pusuit of happiness motivates all our thoughts and actions. It seems to be instinctive, deeply rooted in our nature... in the evolution.

But... the driving force of the Darwinian evolution is the "survival of the fittest". It is the brutal process of the selection, of the merciless elimination of the "weaklings" in favour of the stronger, fitting better in its scheme. It seems to contradict the basic need for fulfilment, implanted in the very nature of life. Is the evolution sadistic?

For millions of years it reigned supreme in the world's wild jungles, and later it insinuated itself into cultural traditions of human race.

Hitler and his followers had based their diabolical ideology and their justification of the holocaust on Darwinian theory of evolution. "We are the super-race," - they proclaimed - "we are the bright future of humanity, not Jews and other inferiors."

Stalin and his followers also had acted on the idea, with a slightly different interpretation of "who is superior and deserves to live and who is not".

In the Middle Ages the "holy" crusaders regarded themselves to be the rightful worshippers of their "only one and true God", who created this world for them, not for the witches, heretics and other "infidels".

Today, the Islamic terrorists uphold the infamous tradition under a very similar banner.

Even in our "civilised" society, the breeding of animals for cruel laboratory experiments, the "intensive farming" and other heartless practices are widely accepted, or at least tolerated as "necessary" for our benefits, on account of our more advanced intellectual faculties.

The list is long...

The list of sufferings inflicted on those who are weaker and helpless by those who claim their "superiority" by brute force, driven by their insatiable greed for power. Given the green light to run wild - and the destructive potential of the modern technology - this greed sooner or later will turn our lovely planet into a lifeless globe, aimlessly circling the sun.

And this puts question to the supposed "wisdom" and "creativity" of the Darwinian evolution.

And it also brings forth yet another, urgent question: is there "Somebody" or "something" in this world... a *force* that can stop this fate, that can change the cursed course? A force that can harmonise everyone's vital needs, thus making battles and atrocities unwanted and obsolete? *A Force that can create the world in which no innocent would ever have to suffer?*

The answer came... as if whispered by a voice

not yet recognised, yet strangely familiar:

"Yes. Think of what Terry had said when he spoke of the evolution four years ago. He had mentioned the higher, *spiritual* aspect of it - but he fell short of being more specific."

"What are they?" - I asked.

"The most important one is *love*."

"Love?"

"Yes, Love. Love that originates not in this world of matter, but in another realm of the Greater Reality - like the rays of the sun, coming from the sky and giving life to every plant, animal and human on the earth.

Universal, boundless and timeless, its deepest Truth cannot be squeezed into the tight compartments of man-made ideologies, creeds and dogmas. It is incomprehensible to the scientific inquires, yet it is felt and understood by every living heart.

It has made its presence felt on the earth ages ago: in the heart of a wild tigress, who kills for her food, yet tends to her cubs with the tenderness and intensity of any human mother.

It motivates every act of compassion: of those who pick up the injured from blood-soaked battlefields and care for them... of those who feed starving children in Africa... of those who cuddle the little kitten, abandoned on snow.

The list is long, too...

Love inspires poets, composers, painters and

many others to express the *beauty* that uplifts us in our daily struggles - and also has inspired the nine year old schoolgirl to write her essay.

Love even transforms guilt into the urge to rescue, to amend and to comfort - and the feelings of hurt received into forgiveness.

Love is the source of happiness, so much desired by every living being - and it also has its own needs and desires: it is restless until it fills all hearts with its bliss.

Love never asks: "*who deserves me?*" but asks instead: "*who needs me?*" It hears all cries for help, unheard on this earth and responds to them. No one is ever forgotten. It is the essence of Jesus message.

In the tradition of Mahaya Buddhism, those who postpone their entry into the glorious Nirvana in afterlife in order to free others from sufferings (as one of their mystics said: 'not until the last blade of grass from the earth is saved') are called 'bodhisattvas'."

* * * * *

This thought has evoked in my mind a memory of a story (from a book on religious beliefs, read some time ago) about the legendary Avalokiteshvana. When he saw how great were the sufferings of this earth's creatures, he wept. He wept and wept... his tears flowed and formed the lake. The beautiful lotus flower sprung up from this lake... and opened, revealing Tara, the goddess of the universal compassion *for all living beings.*

Now, I understood: Love is *the force* that can divert the doomed course of the primordial, cold-hearted, miscalculating evolution... as it silently, but steadfastly, tirelessly keeps breaking the narrow boundaries of countless self-interests and harmonises them in the "Happiness for All" goal in every realm of the Great Reality.

It is the source of Hope.

* * * * *

At long last, the rain has stopped its relentless onslaught on our windows. Only faint, rhythmic splashes of drizzle, streaming down the glass panes were now heard.

I fell asleep and had some wondrous dreams, but - unlike Angela - I had no clear recollection of any of them in the morning.

Chapter 5

DREAMS AND REALITIES

Angela, my little sister...who can so vividly remember her dream after a long time... a rather unusual, if not a puzzling dream.

What possibly could has evoked in her sleeping mind the sad image of a kitten freezing to death on snow, when the only memory of a snowy winter - at her tender age of five - was the one of us running across the field with our home-made by Terry sledge, laughing with joy?

Four years later she has added to this dream her imaginary plot (located in a far away country, only known to her from geography lessons at school!) and created the moving, meaningful story.

Will she retain this ability - and her inspiring imagination in ten years time, when she will be nineteen, like I am now and very likely a budding writer?

Or... maybe after having experienced some life disappointments she will become like Molly, so kind and sensitive, but regarding all "flights of fancy" as being no more than the comforting fairy tales?

Or like Terry, inquiring and open-minded, yet careful and reserved when he steps into an uncharted territory?

Or will she be as I am now: curious but still uncertain and sometimes confused?

No, it is not likely for Angela ever to be confused. She also has the clear understanding of what she sees with her physical and her "heart eyes" and has no problem to accommodate both realities in her inner world, where they co-exist in perfect harmony with each other.

* * * * *

In my early years I lacked my sister's understanding and felt very confused. However hard I tried, I could not make out where my recurring dream was coming from and *why* it has been tormenting me for years. As Molly told me later, I used to wake up at night (mercifully, not every night!), screaming with terror since I was a baby.

This was the *only* dream I still remember now clearly, even nineteen years later. The dream that had cast a dark shadow on my otherwise very happy childhood years.

It was not a dream but a *nightmare.*

It always started with a sense of the blissful comfort. I was happy in my small world, enclosed by soft boundary walls. I could bounce off one wall and find myself embraced by one on the other side. It was fun!

No needs, no desires. No curiosity or

knowledge of any other world outside mine. All was perfect in my little home where I lived.

Then suddenly, without warning: bang! A strange, ear-splitting bang that has filled me and my world with terror.

Then: silence. Not a sound. Not even the soft, rhythmic murmur I always heard before. The silence as strange and as terrifying as the bang. And the helpless feeling of suffocation. In panic, I struggled, hitting wildly at the soft walls of my world that now became a prison.

Next... I always woke up in Molly's arms, listening to her comforting whispering to my ear: "It's all right now, Julia... all is well now. This was only a bad dream."

I then fell back to sleep. No more "bad dreams" that night. Not until the next time, another night, when the nightmare returned with a vengeance.

By the time I was eight, my "bad dreams" begun to change: instead of the sense of suffocation I now heard the loud raps from the other side of my world. Someone there was knocking at the door... a small door in the wall that has never been discovered by me before. Knocking and calling my name.

I felt being torn between two conflicting emotions: one of the curiosity and the impulse to respond, and another of a strong, undefined fear. I screamed, moving away from the door... and each time I found myself wide awake, hugged by Molly.

"Why, Mummy, *why*?" - I cried out one night - "Why this bad dream comes again?"

Molly wiped off the tears from her eyes. "I'll tell you why... I will, Julia. Now you are eight year old, it is the time for you to know."

"Tell me, please..."

"Not now, darling. You need to sleep now. I'll tell you tomorrow, when you are back from school."

"You promise?"

"I do. You know that I always keep my promises."

* * * * *

Next day I spent my school hours absent-mindedly. I couldn't wait to be back at home and hear what Molly will tell me.

My mother has kept her promise.

"Julia," - she started - "there is something we have waited for a long time to tell you..." - she stopped for a moment, then continued: "Eight years ago a tragic road accident had happened on the motorway from Bristol to London. The lorry driver has lost the control, veered across the central reservation and hit head-on the car, travelling on the other side. He and the two car's occupants, a middle-aged couple were killed instantly. Their daughter, who at that time was eight months pregnant, also has died in the hospital soon afterwards - but the doctors were fortunate in saving the life of her unborn baby."

"Why you telling me that, Mum?" - I asked.

"Because... because, Julia, you were this baby, the only survivor of the crash."

I felt very confused. "How this could be?" - I cried out - "You are here, Mum... you had not died in the accident! You are my mother!"

"Yes, Julia... I am. And Terry is your father. We are your parents and we love you... but someone else was your birth mother, not me: the young woman who was killed there, on the motorway..."

I understood what Molly was telling me (at that time in 1988 the basic facts of the natural reproduction were no longer a secret to school-age children), but I could not place the pieces of this new information anywhere in my present emotional turmoil. Molly hugged me close in her arms, as she always did when awaking me from my "bad dream".

"Listen, Julia." - she said - "I'll tell you something about me and Terry. When we were married, we both badly wanted to have the family. But after my doctors have told me that I could never have a child, we started inquiring about our chances of adopting one. And soon after we have been informed that there was a baby girl, the road accident's survivor... with no close relatives willing to take care of her. We were told by the agency that her mother was unmarried and no one knew anything about the baby's father."

I listened.

"The only relative the adoption agency were able to contact,"- Molly continued - "was John, your natural grandfather's brother. John lives in Canada. On several occasions he has visited his brother and his family in England. After the accident he took possession of their personal belongings, like letters and other items. He is the one who knows more about your birth mother and her parents.

He also told the agency that he was willing to share his information with us, if we agree. But at that time... we hesitated, postponing the decision until you were old enough to be told. From now on..." - she looked at me seriously - "this decision will be yours, Julia. What do you say to that?"

I too, felt undecided and still confused.

"But you are my Mummy, aren't you?" - I nearly cried.

"I am, darling. Don't ever doubt it! Do you want to know what it was for me and Terry when you came to us? Our world has changed. I no longer felt any pangs of envy at the sight of other parents with their children. You were so tiny... yet, somehow you have managed to fill all those gnawing "empty places" in our hearts and in our lives. We are grateful to you, our 'miracle child', as we used to call you sometimes. We love you... any doubt?"

"No, Mum."

Molly paused, sipped some tea from the table by our settee and embraced me. Her voice was now very soft, almost a whisper: "Julia... we have waited a long time to tell you all that, but your dreams had no patience. As you have started to describe them to me, a pattern has emerged: your blissful time in your mother's belly... the bang, the sound of the crash... the sense of suffocation when your mother's heart has stopped beating and supplying you with the air..."

"What about someone knocking at the door, Mum?"

"I don't know, darling. Possibly in your dream you felt apprehensive about something unknown, so you retreated. But this doesn't matter any more. Dark dreams, like shadows do fade away when exposed to light, once we know where they come from. They will go away now!"

"Thanks, Mum..."

Molly got up from her seat. "Enough for today, Julia. What about going to the garden and see what Terry is doing there?"

Terry was pruning the privet hedge. When he saw us, he dropped his shears, ran across the lawn to the big lime tree and hid behind its trunk.

"Catch me!" - he shouted.

I laughed. I did remember this game, my favourite game with my Dad from the time when I was a toddler. Terry would circle the tree and I would try to catch him, wobbling on my small legs. After one or two dizzy rounds, he would turn back abruptly, tumble down on the lawn with me falling straight into his open arms and giggling.

Now my legs were longer and swifter; catching up with Terry was no problem. And - as he used to do before - he fell down on the grass. I threw my arms around his neck.

"You are my Daddy, aren't you?" - I asked, still in need of more reassurance.

" I am, Julia. And you are my dear daughter. Molly and I love you." - he said, then jokingly wagged his finger at my face. "Don't you ever, ever dare to doubt it!"

The last traces of my doubt had gone.

In the following weeks my "bad dreams" have also drifted away... one by one, into the safe "Vault of Past Memories" in my mind, from which they could be recalled, but were no longer frightening.

* * * * *

Two years later, when I was ten, to my parents' great surprise (and the astonishment of their doctors!) Molly gave birth to the baby girl. Both Molly and Terry found themselves in the seventh heaven and I joined them there, too. Now, I not only had two wonderful parents but also the sweet little sister. Pushing her pram along our street on my walks with Molly was much more joyful than pushing the small pram with my plastic dolly few years ago!

When Molly asked me to choose the baby's name, I resolutely declared: "Angela!"

Why? Because there was something "angelic" about her from the time she was a tiny infant, sleeping in her cot: a sweet, dreamy expression on her face... or what? Something I could not define, but felt.

The baby grew and my feelings started becoming more and more tangible. As soon as Angela was able to smile, she smiled at every person approaching her and also (a little later) started to stretch her tiny arms towards me, Molly, Terry... everybody, including the birds flying in our garden.

As soon as she was able to talk, she begun to tell me stories about the birds: not about sparrows, blackbirds, magpies and pigeons, but about *the other birds*, big and white who played with her. So sensitive at her age, she felt Molly's uneasy concern when she mentioned the subject and she stopped telling her those stories. Instead, I was the one who became her confidential listener.

And I listened to her tales of the white-silvery birds, as big as she was who had noses and mouths like us in place of their beaks, who had arms and legs, but instead of running they flew on their wings over the flowering shrubs, above the treetops and swooped down to dance around her. Each time she touched one of them, her hand went through the bird, like through the air... and that too, was a great fun!

And I listened... sometimes with a touch of a regret: why had I never seen anything as magical as that, when I was Angela's age? Maybe because my nightmares' shadows, lingering around our place even in the bright daytime, have scared away the celestial birds?

Angela has introduced me - or rather, has set ajar for me the little door into her wonderland. I glimpsed a light beyond it. Alluring, fascinating. And very mysterious.

* * * * *

Before long, Lacy came - or rather burst into our house, with her puppyish charm, with her exhilarant playfulness and soon became Angela's foremost object of attraction. One sunny day in our garden, I asked her, half-jokingly, whether she still plays with the big, white birds.

"No." - she replied - "But they are watching us when we play, from there!" - she pointed her finger at the sky and threw the ball on the lawn for Lacy to retrieve it.

Now, I had my parents, my sister and also her tail-wagging, life-loving dog.

My world was filled with sunshine.

No needs - and only fleeting moments of curiosity about the world that had existed in times before I opened my sleepy eyes.

Chapter 6

LEO'S PAINTING

I met Leo at the Art College where we were both studying painting. Leo was a born artist. His favourite subject were the snowy landscapes. He supplemented his tight student budget by selling his designs to the commercial Christmas card printing companies; his cards were quite often the best-selling ones.

The most popular were the cards of the "Merry Christmas!" type: cheerful children sledging downhill, snowballing, making snowmen with the big, red carrots for their noses; Santa Claus on reindeer-drawn sledge, filled with presents; Santa Claus knocking at the door, with the presents overflowing from his bag... all sorts of cards that brought on smiles.

Less popular (but still in great demand!) were the cards of a different nature: white, snowy dream lands, sometimes with the Star of Bethlehem bright on the night sky; sometimes with people walking across the field towards the church, the golden light flowing out from its open door, radiating welcome.

It was very rare for Leo's design to be rejected by a card producer. But one of them was the one I liked best. It has been rejected because "it was not cheerful enough for Christmas, which is the time of joy."

Leo invited me to his studio to see his original work. He lived in his widowed father's house, only a short distance from the college.

Yes, it was true. The image did not evoke the merriment but entirely different feelings: a subtle sense of "something being there", something not clearly defined, only suggested by shapes and colours. Something bright or gloomy? Heart-warming or melancholic? Appealing yet elusive? I was not sure.

It was a large painting, beautifully done in acrylic. No Star of Bethlehem on the overcast sky. Through the narrow opening between the dark, storm-clouds, the flaming, rising (or setting?) sun twilight the vast, snow-bound field.

In the foreground, the lower part of the big spruce tree. One of its branches, bent down to the ground by the weight of snow was sheltering a small animal, its head partly visible in the shadow of the tree. I thought at first it was a rabbit.

"It is a beautiful painting, Leo..." - I uttered.

"Thanks, Julia." - he replied - "In a way, I'm glad it has not been accepted. I've made a mistake by sending them the photo. On reflection, this painting to me is somehow... private, too private for the commercial use. I really don't know *why* I've painted it... I felt a kind of an urge to do it.

Sometimes we feel like that, don't we?"

"Of course we do..." - I confirmed.

I stepped closer to the picture to see it in detail, focusing my attention on the little creature, squatting in the shadow of the tree. It was not a rabbit. It was a cat, a small cat... a kitten. A *black kitten*!

I could not say a word for few long minutes and Leo waited. At last - and hesitating - I stammered out: "It is beautiful... it reminds me of something. I wish Angela could see it..."

"Angela? Is she your younger sister you have told me you have? Is she interested in painting?"

"I'm not sure." - I replied - "She is only ten. But her range of interests is very wide..."

"If so," - Leo said - "she may like to come here to see my picture. What about this weekend? My father will be back home from London where he lectures on ancient history; he has just published his book on the subject. He is a homely type of person, I know he would be glad to meet you and your sister. Could you bring her here this weekend?"

From my home I was driving daily about twenty miles to the college. Yes, I could bring Angela here this weekend - if she wanted to come.

As I had expected, Angela felt enthusiastic about the invitation.

"Oh, yes!" - she exclaimed - "I would love to see your boyfriend's painting! Is he the one who paints Christmas cards?"

"Angela," - I snapped - "Leo is my friend, *not* my boyfriend!"

"Is he not? Not yet?"

I didn't want to reply *"not yet"*, (as this could be too presuming at the time), but I knew that what she sensed was true.

* * * * *

The next Sunday I drove with Angela to Leo's place. In his studio she stared at the painting for a long time, then turned to Leo.

"You know!" - she exclaimed - "I'm so glad you know!"

" I know what?" Leo was baffled.

"You know he rested there on his way to that house! How else could you paint this picture?"

Leo had no idea what she was talking about. There were few things that badly needed to be explained. So, I told Leo about our summer solstice trip to the woods in search of the fern flower five years ago. About Angela's dream that night, a dream that "in some way" linked the legend with her vision of a little kitten, abandoned on the frosty night. And how, four years later, she wrote her school essay, concluding the story.

"This is a strange coincidence..." - uttered Leo - "A very, very strange coincidence..."

But Angela was not at all interested in "strange coincidences". To her, our speculations were empty and pointless. She fixed her gaze on the picture.

"It is exactly as it was." - she said - "I wish I could have a photo of this painting!"

"No problem." - Leo replied, obviously feeling relief at this turning point in our conversation - "Give me a week or two, I'll make a framed print for you."

"Oh, thanks!" - Angela was overjoyed - "I'll have it on the wall in my room!"

* * * * *

Adam (Leo's father) knocked at the door, announcing that our meal was ready.

Adam was not only the well-known history scholar but also an excellent cook at home. As he knew that Angela and I were vegetarians, he prepared for us the course of roasted potatoes, cooked sauerkraut, spiced omelets and fresh salad, followed by his home-baked apple strudel with tea or coffee. It was delicious.

"I'm glad you both like the sauerkraut." - Leo remarked.

This was an exotic dish for us and we loved its taste.

"It was my mother who introduced me to it." - Adam said - "In Poland where she was born, the sauerkraut is one of the traditional dishes. My mother came to England, where she had some relatives, soon after the last war. She was a Jewish refugee, lucky to survive the holocaust. All her family and friends have been killed by the German Nazis. She was a young girl when she came; here she met and married my father..."

Angela listened, she was all ears.

"What I have heard from my mother is a long and very sad story, not the one to entertain my welcome guests." - Adam tried to smile - "For me, probably it has spurred my interest in history. I tried to answer the question: *Why?* Why wars, atrocities, all the sufferings that the human race keeps at inflicting on oneself?

I started my diggings in the early-times history. No, I did not find what I was searching for - but I became absorbed in the tales and myths of the past."

"I am interested in the old legends from Poland." - spoke Angela.

To Adam, the legendary tale of the fern flowering at the time of the summer solstice was quite familiar. Unfortunately, he said, it originates in times when the written words were not yet known. No historical document exists. The legend has been handed down from one generation to another by the word of mouth.

"But it survived," - Adam concluded - "because of its symbolic, very deep and meaningful message."

* * * * *

A few weeks later, on the eve of Angela's tenth birthday Leo drove his car into our drive and rang the door bell. He carried a wrapped parcel, the present for Angela. There was no way to stop Angela from opening it before the time.

It was not a print, but painted in acrylic the smaller version (to fit Angela's bedroom wall) of Leo's first picture. Similar, but not its replica.

From one side of the foreground "something" (hidden beyond the frame) was beaming the golden-tinted light across the field on the spruce tree.

The black kitten was no longer squatting in its shadow. Now, he was making his first tentative steps on the snow towards this brilliant, spell-binding light.

The Light of Hope.

Chapter 7

THE SEVENTH HEAVEN

According to the Chambers Twentieth Century Dictionary, to be "in the seventh heaven" means to be *"in a state of the most exalted happiness - from the Cabbalists, who divided the heaven into seven in an ascending scale of happiness up to the abode of God".*

I had my doubts about dwelling in the "abode of God" (while still being a traveller in this earthly realm, with so many of others who rarely - if ever - have experienced anything "heavenly"), but I would agree with the definition of "the state of the most exalted happiness".

If not a resident in the place of the Ultimate Bliss, I was rather like a vessel, a glass stuck in the sands of an arid desert, into which the Seventh Heaven was pouring its gift of a welcome rain. My glass was too small to contain it all, yet it was full to the brim and overflowing.

That's how I felt when I and Leo became not only "friends", but "close friends"... and also soul-mates.

* * * * *

Leo was now the frequent guest in our house,

especially at weekends. The guest mostly welcomed by my parents, Angela and also by Lacy, who has greeted him the first time as if he already were her life-long pal. One day, Angela (well known for her unreserved openness) said to him: "You are like my brother!"

As Leo looked at her slightly surprised, she added: "You are a *kind* of my brother, because we sometimes think the same way, even if we don't talk. Otherwise, how

did you come to know about the black kitten *before* Julia had told you?"

No one could answer that.

* * * * *

It was easy to like Leo... for his gentle manners and his friendliness. For the passion with which he painted his pictures and lived his life. For his open-mindedness and his integrity.

Before long I discovered that it was also easy to *love* him.

* * * * *

During long summer days, Leo and I used to ramble in our countryside. On those occasions, Angela - as always, so sensitive and understanding - refused to come with us, but she gracefully allowed us to take Lacy, "her" dog on our walks. And of course, Lacy also demanded to go by her excited barks!

Often we climbed through the woods to the wide, open grassland on the top of the hill which, like a peninsula, sloped steeply on three sides, revealing the bird's eye views of the villages and fields below, and the river Severn in the west, few miles away.

One sunny afternoon we decided to go there to watch the sunset from the hilltop. It was there, waiting for us to see it in all its splendour.

The flaming, setting sun was casting its light on the serpentine course of the river. The drifting fog took in the glow and scattered it all around, turning the valley into the misty sea of the golden-reddish radiance. It also has reached us, standing on the hilltop, snuggled in the gleaming, all-embracing mist and becoming a part of the wondrous landscape... a part of the new, yet unknown world, where time was flowing at a different pace: it was no longer evening, but *a dawn*... a dawn of the Great Hope and Promise, which had no patience to wait through the night and had to break in now!

We kissed, and we kissed... no idea for how long - till Lacy has brought us back to our "usual", everyday world with her loud barking.

"I am here!" - she shouted in her dog language - "It is getting dark! Time to go home for the supper!"

We walked back downhill along the woodland path, Lacy ahead of us. Suddenly she stopped and looked ahead, sniffing. Few yards away, another creature was standing there, watching her. It was a fox.

No one chased the other, no one was running away. They were both just curious of each other.

"Friend or foe?" - the fox seemed to ask, judging from his posture. It was clear that he found it difficult to make up his mind. Slowly, very slowly Lacy dropped down to the ground, her tail wagging. This has puzzled the fox, making his decision to "run or fight" not only difficult, but impossible. Seconds, or minutes had passed.

Lacy - still very slowly - started to crawl towards the fox.

"Play with me!" - she pleaded silently with her every movement. But the fox (maybe after some consideration?) has decided that this kind of familiarity was rather premature. He backed away few steps, gave Lacy the last, long look, then turned and disappeared in the nearby bushes. Lacy stood up, sniffing the air, her tail still wagging - as if hoping that the fox would come out again.

He did not, so she decided to follow us downhill. Disappointed, her head and tail down.

I cuddled her. "Oh, Lacy!" - I said - "You didn't know that foxes are too shy to play with dogs!"

There were more bushes at the side of the path and there, on the bottom grew few tall, majestic ferns. We stopped there, relaxing after a long climb-down. A thought, a wish came to my mind: if "somehow" it could be possible to make the time to flow back to the night of the summer solstice... would I see it now, the elusive Mystery Flower?

Leo embraced me. "I know what you are thinking." - he whispered - "And we know it does exist... out of our view now, but not invisible. We are on the journey to find it... on *our journey, Julia.*"

* * * * *

Few months later, Leo and I became a married couple. It was a quiet event. As both of us were shy of the great, loud ceremonies, hardly anyone had noticed it, except for those close to us.

Thanks to the helpful generosity of my parents and Adam, we were able to get the mortgage to buy a lovely, old cottage at the end of a country lane near the woods and only a walking distance from my parents house. On one side, our large orchard bordered on the woodland, on another on the pasture where the cattle was grazing. Sometimes a cow would come close to our wooden fencing, as if saying "Hallo!" to us - and sometimes a deer from the wood would jump over it for the feast of fallen apples on our lawn. Each morning we woke up to the chirping sound of the birds' chorus, singing out their joy of living.

* * * * *

The "Seventh Heaven"? If this meant to be the

"*Ultimate* Bliss", it was something beyond the scope of our limited, human imagination. But we felt our happiness, we knew it, we experienced it with every cell of our beings... like the vessels in the sand, overflowing with the gifts from the very kind and generous Sky... full to their brims.

Chapter 8

OLIVER

The world around us was one vast, white dreamland under the soft embrace of the deep snow when Oliver came into it: the cute, rosy-cheeked baby boy, our son. Another gift from the Seventh Heaven.

By that time (soon after we both had graduated from the Art College) Leo established his own, independent greeting cards' production business. We transformed our large garage into the printing shop and one room in the house into his studio. I was doing most of the secretarial tasks. The business was flourishing. We were able to stay most of the time at home to be with our new-born child.

Angela and (of course!) Lacy were often more residents than guests in our place, also Molly, Terry and Adam were our frequent visitors. Everyone was helping us as much as they could. Everyone wanted to see and to cuddle our baby and to talk about him. Angela loved to rock him in her arms and sing her promptly improvised lullaby.

As it had happened twelve years ago, when Molly let me to choose my little sister's name, so now I asked Angela to do the same for our son. And

- with the same absence of any hesitation she stated: "Oliver!"

"It is a lovely name," - I said - "and rather unusual. As far as I can remember, it originates from the word 'olive'. In the ancient Greece the olive branch was the symbol of peace."

"Yes, Julia." - Angela replied - "That's why this name - and not any other - came to my mind!"

* * * * *

Years went by... how privileged I felt (for the second time in my life!) to witness, to watch one of the greatest miracle of the Nature: the feeling, thinking and active human being growing out of a small bunch of living flesh! And I watched... and thought and wondered... till all my thinking and wondering got lost in the great complexity of Life's enigma. What was left was my love and my joy of being so close to the Mystery that allowed us to catch a glimpse of it: the reflection of lights, dancing on its surface, while its depths still remained unfathomable to us. Not because of any "No Entry" sign over there, but because we failed as proficient divers.

* * * * *

As a toddler, Oliver was brimming with the enthusiastic interest in everything he touched and saw: a cloud drifting across the sky... leaves swayed by a breeze... the reflection of his face in the garden pool's water (then, he would laugh and clap his hands, delighted to see his mirrored "other self" mimicking his movements!)... birds flying down from the trees for the feast at their feeder...

Birds... sometimes, for a moment my heartbeat would quicken: will he - as Angela did in her childhood years - start telling me the stories about the *other* fowls of the air? But he didn't. He has quickly learned the names of sparrows, crows, blackbirds, tits, magpies, robins... all birds that could be seen by everyone of us, only those birds.

Will Angela during her visits to play with him in our garden tell him her fairy-tales? But she did not.

Molly had no reason to be concerned about the state of her grandson's mental perception. Oliver seemed to be firmly rooted in our solid reality and fully enjoying it. No puzzling dreams, no visions... not until he was five, on that one winter day.

* * * * *

It was like the day when Oliver was born. Winter... a continental type of winter, on one of its rare visit to the British shores. Frost and snow. Snow... cascading from the sky for hours at a stretch, eager to reshape our green and grey January countryside into the vast, all-white, softly outlined landscape - to the great delight of the painters (like Leo) and sledging and snowballing children, but not to the delight of drivers stranded on our un-gritted country roads.

We were just lucky with no need to travel for few days. Angela came with Lacy; journeying along the snowbound country lanes was no problem for walkers! However, it took her longer than usual, as Lacy, now fourteen year old could no longer run or jump, only to tread her way through the snow slowly, yet (according to what Angela said) enjoying her every step.

Oliver was first at the door to greet them. "Look!" - he exclaimed, indicating a single snowflake on Angela, glove.

I looked. A snowflake, "just" a snowflake... but, when viewed closely, it revealed its (rarely noticed and appreciated) fascinating aspect: the perfect symmetry of its exquisite design, unique for every existing snowflake... and there were millions, trillions of them all around us!

Angela did not take off her gloves, as Oliver pulled her into the living room. There, after a minute or two in the warm place the little snowflake became a drop of water, then evaporated. Oliver looked disappointed. "It is gone!" - he whispered sadly.

Angela opened the window and with her gloved hand pointed at the sky.

"It is gone there!" - she said - "And it'll come back from the cloud... as long as it is still very cold outside!"

Oliver listened, pondering. "So... it will never be back in the summer?"- he asked.

"No. But there are many, many snowflakes on the field now. Shall we go there... after the lunch?"

That cheered Oliver up.

Chapter 9

KOTECK

Snow has stopped falling in the afternoon. Oliver could no longer catch and admire a single snowflake. But he soon has forgotten it, now excited by a new joy.

Our back garden was bordering on the vast pasture land that sloped up gently to the edge of the woods. The ideal place for sledging. We took with us our old sledge, made by Terry fifteen years ago for Angela and me, still in the perfect condition - it was Angela's gift to Oliver.

And... downhill we went! First, Leo with Oliver in front of him, then Oliver with me, Oliver with Angela, then... whoever wanted another exhilarating ride to the bottom of the hill! Except for Lacy who preferred to stay on the top, each one of us wanted it, sometimes everyone at the same time! Leo has promised to make another sledge, ready for us to use in the next snowy winter, whenever it may come - and Terry will tell him how to make it.

One or two hours have passed. It was time to return home.

We had to wait for Lacy, who was now busy sniffing something around the big tree at the edge of the field and refused to come, but responded to our calls with loud, urging barks. Oliver run to her. Angela, Leo and I followed him.

Lacy was trying to squeeze under the big bough of the tree which was heavy, weighed down to the ground by snow. She failed, so she started digging a tunnel in the snow.

"He is here!" - Oliver shouted.

I had no idea who was "he", but we soon have found out when Angela lifted the bough.

There "he" was. Sheltered by the wide tree's trunk, trembling with cold, uttering feeble, plaintive mews... the little black kitten.

Angela knelt down on the snow and lifted the half-alive, small furry thing into her arms. Lacy moved close to her and started licking the kitten, from the top of his head to his tail - at first slowly and gently, then more vigorously... until he started purring with contentment. Angela placed the kitten into the little nest, made from the top of her unbuttoned winter coat and got on her feet.

Tears were running down her face, like an overflowing stream, irresistible and unrestrained.

"Julia," - she whispered to me - "It is just like it was in my dream."

Yes. It was like in her dream, twelve years ago.

We walked back home in silence.

*****

The old, big sofa in our dining room served well as the place to rest and to sleep for both the kitten and Lacy who insisted on staying close to her new feline pal and treated him as if he were her own puppy. Another sofa was turned into the bed for Angela who wanted to keep her eye on them in the same room.

I phoned our parents to tell them that Angela with Lacy would stay with us tonight - and I explained why.

The kitten recovered quickly from his ordeal. He drank some milk, nibbled a morsel of Lacy's food and settled in the sofa, cuddling close to the dog.

"How are we going to name him?" - I asked.

"Koteck!" - exclaimed Oliver.

"Do you mean 'Kitten'?" - I inquired, thinking that my very young son has simply mispronounced the word.

"No, no!" - Oliver shouted out - "I know that he *is* the kitten, but his name *is* Koteck! That was his name *before* he came to us!"

* * * * *

No one has asked him more questions. Angela didn't seem to be surprised at all.

"OK, Oliver." - she said - 'Koteck' is a nice name. I like it!" She turned to Leo and me: "Do you like it, too?"

We nodded, assenting.

* * * * *

The next morning greeted us with sunshine and the warm air, blown by the southerly wind. The rapidly thawing snow allowed the green patches of grass to appear on lawns and fields and turned the roads into slushy, brownish tracks, quite ugly but more accessible to drivers.

Our Koteck looked today more like a normal, happy pussy then like the sad, barely alive creature, found yesterday. With Oliver and Lacy he explored the garden, stepping carefully on the grass and avoiding the snowy patches, then followed Lacy back to the house, as any other kitten who likes to stay close to his mum would do. It didn't take him long to feel at home with us.

* * * * *

Leo drove around, asking people about someone who may have lost a little black kitten.

"No result." - he announced on his return - "No one knows anything about a black - or any other kitten in his neighbourhood."

I could not make out whether he felt disappointed, or relieved, or puzzled, or... what else? But he no longer talked about the "strange coincidences". Instead he mentioned something that he read in a book a year or two ago: something about "parallel universes".

"Terry will know more about it." - he said.

Molly and Terry - with the welcome bag of the cat food - came to us in the early afternoon.

"Parallel universes?" - Terry spoke - "Yes. Today, many quantum physics scientists regard them as indisputably real. This is the logical conclusion drawn from the results of their verified research experiments. To someone who considers those results from our 'common' point of view, they seem to be puzzling and unbelievable - yet, they make sense to those who accept the postulated theory of the one, great, multi-dimensional Universe.

We are living in the four-dimensional universe (three of space and one of time), and to our habitual thinking the idea of yet another dimension is alien and unimaginable. To use a rough illustration: let's assume that we are dwellers of an even more primitive, three-dimensional world (one of time and only two of space) - a kind of a flatland where we know 'forth and back', 'left and right', but have no idea about any 'up and down'. When one day (however rarely!) something drops in from the world above us, we feel surprised and call it 'unusual event', or 'vision', or 'miracle'.

"Thanks, Terry." - Leo said - "You've clarified the subject so well. Much better that what I used to think about it in my childhood years. I loved the fairy tales and often dreamt of 'another world', as wonderful and exciting as the one described by them.

My grandmother, who comes from Poland has often sung for me her Polish songs. I've learned some of her native language and listened to poems she recited. I loved them, too. Especially those written by the Polish poet, Adam Mickiewicz. I translated into English few of my favourite verses, like those:

'Reach out to what lies beyond vision,
Find out what the reason can't find...'

This has captivated my imagination. I fantasised that I was the inhabitant of a far away, isolated island. People living there knew nothing about other islands. They only saw the ocean around them, as far as they could explore it in their small boats. To them, the horizon line demarcated the boundaries of the world. I was a sailor there. One day I ventured alone into the sea farther than ever before. And there, I spotted a boat in the distance... unlike any other boat I've seen. I stared at it... but after few minutes the boat disappeared beyond the horizon.

Back on the island, I told others what I had seen. They laughed at me: 'Don't be silly. No one else sails in our waters. There is no other land but ours.'

Yet, I still kept at dreaming of this mysterious boat and where it came from... when I was young."

"Yes, Leo!" - Terry exclaimed - "It is wonderful that in all times and places there are always dreamers with the passion to discover and to chart uncharted lands... those beyond the horizon line!"

"Dad," - I asked - "do you think that what you've said could throw more light on what had happened in Koteck's story?"

"Yes, I do. I do because this finds some missing pieces of our jigsaw puzzle. The puzzle of Angela's childhood dream. The puzzle of how Leo, few years later - and with no prior knowledge of it - has rendered in acrylic the image of her dream... and how now, in our material reality, the recent events reflect those dreams and inspiration.

It does make sense. To those with a narrow point of view, a kitten (like the one from Angela's school essay) might have died in some place and time - and that's the end of the story. But to those who see things from a wider perspective, his 'essence' or 'soul' (the vital part of every living being), once liberated from the matter, can find home in another universe - and it also can return to our world in the new, physical form. Unlike bodies, souls can travel very far..."

"Reincarnation?" - I asked.

"It could be what we call it." - replied Terry - "As the results of the quantum physics experiments show, the parallel universes are not isolated. They can communicate, influence and even interact with each other. There are *bridges*... invisible, subtle, yet very effective bridges of contact."

"What do you think," - Leo asked - "is what

gives us the access to them?"

"It is the power of the mind." - Terry said - "The power of some deep thoughts and emotions: creativity, inspired by sense of beauty. Deeply felt heart desires. Grief, crying out for reunion. Guilt, crying out to make amends. Suffering that cries out for help. Prayers. Longings to reach out beyond restrictive limitations. And love... the most powerful way of contact.

We underestimate the power of our thoughts and feelings. But they can 'move mountains', as Jesus has said."

Terry paused for a moment and continued: "That's what I think has happened here. A contact." - He turned to Angela with a smile: "You, my dear daughter, seem to live in the close neighbourhood of one of those bright contact bridges!"

"Not only me, Dad. Also Leo... and now, Oliver."

"True. It looks that what makes its way to us can also spread around and affect others in our family group... like tiny seeds, blown by the wind or carried on butterflies wings."

"I don't feel affected!" - Molly protested - "Look, Terry. What you have said could be very interesting... for poets and dreamers. But I am living in my 'limited' four-dimensional reality. My mind gets overloaded and confused, trying to grasp something beyond it!

However, just out of curiosity: what do you

think happened to Koteck *before* our sledging team has found him on the field? Another mystery? Or... I would propose a simpler explanation: someone who lives far away, farther than the range of your inquiry, Leo, wanted to get rid of the cat, brought him here by car and left at the edge of the wood. From there the kitten came downhill to the field and found shelter from the suddenly outbreaking snow-storm under the big tree. This would explain all."

"Not all, Mum." - I denied - "Not why Angela has dreamed of it twelve years *before*... and why Leo has painted the scene... just as we have found it yesterday!"

"What else will?" - Molly replied - "Telepathy? Precognition? I know nothing about them, so I call them 'unknown'. Anyway... what we do know is the happy ending of an otherwise sad story." - She now addressed Oliver, who looked bored listening to what he could not quite understand - "I like the name you gave to this kitten, 'Koteck'!"

At that moment Koteck decided to come off his seat close to Oliver and jump on Molly's lap.

"What a clever little pussy!" - Molly said - "He already knows his name!" - She fondled the kitten - "I'm so glad that you've found him... in *our universe*!" - she added with a smile.

Chapter 10

SNOWFLAKE

Angela was now eighteen, the student of philology at the university in London, where she spent most of her time. During her absence from home Lacy used to stay with us, so she could enjoy Koteck's company. In the garden they have invented their game: Koteck trying to catch Lacy's wagging tail when she was lying on the grass - Lacy getting up and hobbling (not running at her age of fifteen!) around the lawn - Koteck jumping up, trying to catch the flying above her tail, and so on... till Lacy dropped on the ground panting, her tail no longer wagging incitingly. At night they slept together in the dog bed, cuddled up to each other.

* * * * *

In her spare time Angela wrote stories, published in children books and magazines. The stories full of adventures and surprises that kept her readers interested and waiting for more... and the stories (also desired by many!) in which the events were happening sometimes in our world and sometimes in another, beautiful and mysterious dream-land.

Mountains and valleys, lakes and rivers were in

this land; trees and flowers grew there, more resplendent than anything we've ever seen or even imagined to be. People and animals were living there, all friendly and playful. Sun was shining, birds were singing lovely, melodious songs.

Angels also lived in this world and from time to time they visited our place here: the little angels who loved to play with human toddlers in their gardens - and the bigger, invisible angels who whispered good advises into people's ears... and left them wondering where all those "bright ideas" came from.

And they were bridges from this land to us, living here: the long rainbow bridges for visiting angels and for the refugees from the earth who had suffered there and badly needed solace, a ray of comfort... and love.

One of the stories she wrote has been printed (but not published) especially for Oliver, as the present for his sixth birthday. In the twenty pages of the booklet, entitled "Snowflake" Angela described how the life of a young boy, named Owen has been influenced by one event in his childhood: how one day in the winter the boy noticed a snowflake, lying alone on the outside sill of his bedroom window. He didn't touch it. He was a wise boy and he knew that if someone reaches out for it, the flake would vanish into thin air. He just looked at it through the window's glass every morning.

The warm weather came. All snow was gone - except for one little snowflake on Owen's bedroom window, which refused to thaw and stayed in its place, white and bright - throughout the spring and the early summer.

One night - it was the night of the summer solstice, twenty-first of the June - Owen woke up, hearing some strange rustle on his window. The snowflake was moving! Moving, rustling, growing and changing its shape... till it became the silvery butterfly. It fluttered its wings and flew into the garden. The boy got up and followed the shining trail left by its flight, to the end of the orchard where a tall fern grew. The butterfly alighted on the fern's highest twig.

It rested there for a while, then started moving again. Still holding to the fern's twig, it began to turn round, slowly at first, then faster and faster... pirouetting to the tune of a lively, swift melody... and still faster, whirling dizzily, till all that could be seen was a shimmering cloud, sparkling with a riot of colours.

Suddenly, the movements slowed down and stopped. All was still, no sound. On the top of the fern bush the big, beautiful flower came into view. More beautiful than anything known in this world. It was here, no longer elusive and invisible.

It had the splendour that did not dazzle or overawe the onlooker. It radiated welcome. Owen stood and looked at it, he didn't know for how long... minutes or hours?

Slowly, very slowly the flower's petals lifted, but didn't close into the bud. Instead, they grew long... longer and longer, stretching upwards, soaring to the night sky... their colours falling into bright-hued bands and forming a rainbow... the glowing rainbow bridge between the earth and everything that lies beyond it.

All of a sudden, a gust of wind blew a dark cloud across the sky, hiding the rainbow from sight. Its lower end, still touching the earth, gradually faded away, leaving shining dew drops on the grasses, trees... and on the fern, now displaying its tall twigs and leaves... *only the leaves.*

Owen walked back to the house, his heart and mind filled with the memory of what he had witnessed. Now, he knew that there are more wonders hidden in snowflakes, butterflies, flowers, rainbows and many other things... the wonders we don't always see.

* * * * *

Oliver has allowed us (everyone in our family but no-one else) to read the story. He hardly ever parted with his booklet, even kept it under his pillow at night.

"Angela," - I spoke to her - "I love it! Please, keep at writing your stories. They are needed and awaited by many!"

"That's what I want to do, Julia." - she replied -

"But sometimes..."

"Sometimes, what?"

"Sometimes I feel as if... as if a storm was brewing."

"Steer clear of it, Angela. Stay close to your bridge!"

"I will, Julia..." - she whispered and said no more.

I could not guess what she meant by "brewing storm" - but before long the answer came, uninvited.

Chapter 11

A BROKEN BRIDGE

Malcolm, Angela's first boyfriend, was also a writer - of a different kind. His first published book, entitled "The Swimmer" was a tale of the life of his hero, Victor who from his early childhood loved swimming: in the sea and lakes in summer and in the swimming pool, available in all seasons, in any weather. There was another excitement there: the competition. Victor has discovered the joy of winning and "being better than the others". He won a lot of prices in the local swimming contests, and later many gold medals in the Olympic games. He was brimming over with the pride of his achievements.

In his real life, Malcolm also won medals in several swimming events - but not as many as his book's hero did. He was more successful in another field: his handsome looks and charming manners easily attracted - and often won the young girls' hearts. Angela was one of them.

In London, away from us and everything she loved, Angela felt estranged and isolated. Malcolm has provided a refuge from her loneliness.

They met at a gathering of the young writers' club. Malcolm was serious this time. He fell in love with Angela... if not quite with all her stories; he thought they were "very interesting and well written, but rather far-fetched". Angela has heard similar comments more than once before, she was used to them. But the romantic love was something new - and she was a born explorer.

Angela also loved swimming - in the sea, on our daylong trips to the Dorset coast in summer. Especially when she and Lacy (in her younger age) were competing in the race to retrieve a stick thrown by one of us into the waves. They both came out of the water exhilarated and happy, regardless of who was the winner and who the looser. That was what Angela thought of competition: to her it was the joy of swimming, splashing and riding breaking waves... with no one left disappointed at the end of the game. However, she accepted that Malcolm did not feel the same way.

To please her, Malcolm proposed a holiday together in Greece, where they both could swim to their hearts' content under the blue sky of the Mediterranean Sea.

"Don't worry about Lacy." - I told Angela, feeling her concern - "Yes, she is old and frail, but still very healthy for her age. She will be happy here with Koteck. She will just wait for you to return, as she did when you were in London."

I think I convinced Angela. They departed in the early September.

* * * * *

Alas, this time it was not as it used to be before. The next day after Angela's departure, Lacy became restless. She would pace the room up and down, then lie by the front door, uttering the whimpering, broken cries, as if asking: "Where are you?" - unresponsive to my caresses and to Koteck's invitations to play.

I thought a short walk may cheer her up, and off we went. As soon as we came round the corner, Lacy stood still and refused to move, sniffing the air, her head turned in one, fixed direction. I drew an imaginary line along it: it ran straight south-east; if extended, it would mark the flight route from here to Greece. Eventually, Lacy decided to return home, her head and tail down.

How dogs know where their masters are? I heard the stories of dogs (and cats), finding their way home from the distance of a hundred or more miles. If their (keen, but now insufficient) sense of smell failed, they simply would use their "other Sense". In our case, the distance was about two thousand miles. It would be hopeless to attempt that journey and Lacy was aware of that. But she knew where Angela was.

Next day Lacy didn't want to go for a walk. And no longer she walked up and down the room or cried. She just lied in her bed, sometimes lifting her head and looking at me with the tired, sad eyes.

And she refused to eat.

We called the vet. He said that she was "just pining" and he could not prescribe any medication. He looked sad. I could guess what he was thinking: that these were Lacy's last days.

Angela phoned the same evening. While I was searching my mind, trying to find the way to soften the hard news, she announced: "I'm coming back!" And she did - as soon as she was able to catch the first flight to London.

* * * * *

Lacy revived. No end of her wet kisses on Angela's face, no end of her excited screams of joy... of the overwhelming, overflowing joy that was unable to restrain itself from bursting out... of the sheer ecstasy of their reunion. No end of soft words, whispered by Angela into Lacy's ears... the words they both understood well.

That night Angela slept in our guest room, with Lacy cuddled close to her. Somehow, Koteck has found a place for himself there, too.

* * * * *

Angela stayed with us in the following days. Nothing on earth could separate her from Lacy - or Lacy from her. Lacy was now Angela's shadow, following her everywhere in the house and in the garden... sometimes wobbling, yet with her tail wagging... still wagging, but with the slower and slower movements. We all knew why.

Can the sadness be peaceful? Instead of being the agonising struggle for survival, can it accommodate a calm acceptance? Acceptance, not the resignation that equals nothingness, but the kind of acceptance which is filled with the comforting certainty that "all is well" when one feels being loved? That the best thing to do at the moment is to sleep and dream, while basking in this love?

I could answer "yes" to those questions. Because I knew this was what Lacy was feeling now. All she wanted was to sleep and stay close to Angela. And... now and then - however feebly - to wag her tail.

*****

Malcolm stayed in Greece till the end of his scheduled holiday. As soon as he returned, he was at our door, asking to see Angela. He was not in the best mood.

"You've spoiled our holiday!" - he accused.

"Lacy needed me... she is dying." - Angela replied.

"Oh!" - Malcolm tried to control his anger - "It is always sad when a pet dies. But... your Lacy is very old, she had her life. After all, she is only a dog..."

"No, Malcolm!" - now, it was Angela who raised her voce - "Lacy is more than 'only a dog' to me!"

"If that's how you feel..." Malcolm's words became softer, almost pleading - "Look, Angela: I love you. We were planning our life together. I've already started looking for a house to buy. I don't mind if you want another dog. But... Angela, please tell me: how can I compete for your love... with your dog?"

Angela looked at him and spoke in a serious tone, spelling her every word: "You don't have to, Malcolm."

Malcolm did not reply. He got up and left. After he has closed the door, Lacy did something she has never done in her long life: she growled.

* * * * *

Oliver loved stories and films about animals. That evening we watched the recorded TV documentary about elephants' life in the sun-scorched African savannah. Only one big tree, still leafy, grew there, offering a refuge from heat and leaves to eat. The herd of elephants were dozing in its welcomed shadow.

A group of wild goats arrived. They all started eating leaves from the tree's lowest branches - all, except for one, not fully grown kid, who found impossible to reach them. Desperately, he kept at jumping up - to no effect.

One elephant has noticed that. With his long trunk he pulled the bough down and held it low while the kid enjoyed its meal.

"This elephant has the good heart!" - remarked Oliver at the end of the film.

"Yes," - Angela said - "Many animals have good hearts."

"And Koteck, and Lacy?"

"Yes, Oliver. And Koteck... and Lacy..." - Angela answered. Oliver sensed that she was in no mood to talk and he asked no more questions.

* * * * *

Lacy was sleeping with her head on Angela's lap. I switched on the recorder to play a soft, relaxing music - the one which Angela and also Lacy always loved to hear. Lacy responded: she looked at me, wagged her tail once and fell asleep again.

"I'll stay with you, Angela." - I said. Leo and Oliver (with Koteck in his arms) went upstairs to their bedrooms.

Angela was stroking Lacy, humming softly to the tune of the played melody. Lacy slept.

"She will not wake up now..." - Angela murmured.

It was true. No more waking up. No more wagging tail. No more running and barking. No more... in this world.

* * * * *

It was hard. Very hard for each one of us in our family to learn how to live without Lacy. The hole.

The gaping, dark emptiness. Her empty bed, in which Koteck no longer wanted to sleep. Her empty bowl, from which no one wanted to eat. The empty silence that followed the ringing of the door bell - instead of the usual sound of her excited barking. Empty shadows in the garden where Lacy used to run...

Koteck was looking for her in every room, in every place where he thought she might be hiding - and after each fruitless search uttering sorrowful mews.

Oliver kept asking me questions to which I could find no answers.

We all missed Lacy.

* * * * *

Angela, my younger sister - yet otherwise more mature, with her wisdom of things not quite comprehensible to me... will she, like the rest of us, wait and hope for the merciful passage of time to heal the most painful wounds?

She did not. Her grief was as deep as an abyss and her heart sang into it.

She wrote the poem and read it to me:

"*WHERE ARE YOU?*

Starry night, clear and peaceful. Late summer.
Time to go for a walk, though alone...
As we used to go, always together

Through the streets and the footpaths well known.
But the place is no longer familiar,
Stars not bright, trees and houses all changed...
With no one sniffing corners and bushes
The great world is so empty. Cold. Strange.

Sky above, vast and distant. Trees' branches
Cast dark shadows on moonlit, cold stones...
"Here you were, with your joy of exploring,
Sparkling eyes, wagging tail, muddy paws!"

Against reason comes question that shatters
Deadly silence of this lonely walk:
"You are not here, beside me... where are you?
Where you are... my dear friend, my lost dog?"

Those who know what the life is: an endless
Search for meaning, for joy and for love,
Found and lost... and yet never forgotten
In this world so confused, harsh and sad,

They (like me) will keep asking questions
Unresolved by the logics of thought,
Chasing dreams, bits of hope... chasing shadows,
Searching, calling: 'Where are you, my dog?' "

"Thanks, Angela." - I said - "That's how I feel, too. Thanks! You know... the pain seems to be less - at least a little less stinging when it is expressed."

"Julia," - Angela spoke in a low voice - "now, for the first time in my life, I know what the real pain is."

I was waiting for her to explain.

"I also feel that I *needed* to know." - Angela said.

"Why?"

"Julia... my life, from its very beginning was easy, filled with blessings. I was loved by my parents and by you. I had everything I needed to dance with pleasure. My happiness attracted little angels from the Heaven and I danced with them. And with sun-rays, with flowers and leaves, swayed in the wind... I danced with life.

My first encounter with the suffering came when I was three... do you remember? When we heard Lacy screaming in pain, beaten by Karl. This was new, this was strange... it didn't belong to *my* world I knew. It was something coming from the outside and hitting me, something awful. All I wanted was to stop it... to stop it! You've done it, Julia. We took Lacy home and she was happy. Everything was back as it has been before, as the things should be. I understood that if they were not, you just have to stop them and all is well again! Only much later in my life I've learned that not everything is always as simple as that."

"That's true, Angela. That's how life is..."

"What I've experienced then, Julia," - she continued - "was the suffering of someone else, not mine. Maybe I needed to feel it myself. Whether I liked it or not, someone - or something deep inside me wanted me to know what the raw, helpless grief is... as it is felt by those who are not aware of the existence of any other world but the one they can recognise by sight, touch and hearing.

This grief is like a storm, hurricane that sweeps and breaks everything in its way - and blows in the dark cloud which overshadows my world. My bridge, Julia.. *my bridge is broken..."*

"Angela," - I said - "being out of sight is not the same as being broken!"

"True. It could be that my fear is suggesting the worst scenario. Fear likes to accompany the sorrow. It is powerful, it can kill Hope. I can sense it in people... and in animals."

"In places where you do your voluntary work for the animal charity?"

"Yes." - Now, Angela started telling me the stories: about dogs and cats, abandoned, neglected, abused and even tortured by people... but she couldn't continue. She burst into tears.

"What I do," - she stammered between the sobs - "is a drop in the huge ocean of sufferings. Sufferings of those who don't even know what hope is. That's why I cry."

* * * * *

The memories suddenly flooded into my mind: the memories from the time fourteen years ago, when at night I thought of the Buddhist tale of how Tara, the goddess of universal love and compassion has emerged from the lotus flower that grew in the lake - the lake of tears, shed by the legendary Avalokiteshvana, who wept when he saw how great were the sufferings of the living beings on the Earth.

* * * * *

I told Angela this story - and she smiled.

Chapter 12

SYLVIA'S MEMORIES

One day Molly came to our house, carrying the large envelope.

"It is addressed to us, - she said - "but I think it is you Julia, who should be the first to open it."

I took the packet in my hands, looked at the unfamiliar postage-stamps and the address of the sender. It was from Robert West in Canada.

"Mum," - I said - "I don't know any Robert West!"

"Neither I do." - Molly replied - "But it is from Canada, where John West, your natural grandfather's brother lives. It may concern something you need to know."

Somehow hesitatingly, I opened the envelope. It contained the letter on the top of yet another envelope.

I read the letter. Robert West was the son of John West. John has died recently, aged eighty-three. He was the widower. In the pile of his letters and documents Robert has found some of the correspondence with Molly and Terry, my parents, thirty years ago.

Thirty years ago... when my birth mother and her parents were killed in the road accident... when the only crash survivor was the yet-unborn baby in the mother's womb, saved by the doctors. When I was this baby... Molly told me all about it when I was eight year old - and I promptly relegated the story to the deep, dark recess in my mind. My life was great as it was, with Molly and Terry, the only parents I knew. No need to find out about another family, who even didn't exist in the world I loved, the world familiar to me.

Robert's letter contained more information: the names of my birth mother, Eva, and of her parents, Eric and Sylvia. And also of what John told his son in the last year of his life: he told him that Sylvia, my ancestral granny, few months before her tragic death had started writing the memoirs of her life. They were enclosed in the inner envelope of the letter. As I was the only one left from Sylvia's blood family, Robert felt that they should belong to me.

Something was now welling up from the dark depth of my memory... like someone knocking at the door of my tiny world in my mother's womb, in my childhood dreams... someone who desperately wanted to tell me something...

Can I, again barricade my entrance door?

I opened the inner envelope and started reading my granny's memoirs.

They were hand-written, their pages yellowing with age.

This is what Sylvia wrote:

Rather late in my life (I'm fifty!) I decided to write about some events of my past - the events that stay in my memory still fresh after so many years. Many times I wanted to tell Eva about them - but somehow we never had that time. Life was so busy. And Eva was also very busy, working in London, about a hundred miles away from where I live now with Eric, my husband. Something (I don't know what) keeps at prompting me to write. Maybe Eva, later in her life will be more interested.. or her child? Eva told us that she is expecting. Both Eric and I feel excited and look forward to see our grandchild... boy or girl? I have a feeling (again, I don't know why) it will be a girl. We are planning to go to London and stay with Eva for some time, to help her with the baby. Eva is a single mother.

I'll start with the most vivid memories from my early years.

I was born in Poland. I was six year old when the Second World War broke out in September, 1939. My father joined the Polish army - to defend us from Hitler. The life was hard for my mother and me, her only child. Hard and terrifying. Even now, after so many years, sometimes the sound of a passing overhead passenger plane at night awakes me from sleep: I can still hear the dreaded, deafening roar of war aircraft and the bangs of exploding bombs.

In our (very primitive, hurriedly dug in the garden by my mother and our neighbours) underground shelter, my mother usually started to pray out loud and everyone chimed in with her. When the bombing has stopped, we thanked God for being alive. I was very scared and I prayed from the bottom of my heart.

Our next-door neighbours were the Jewish couple with two daughters, only two years older than me, Rachel and Sara. They were the identical twins, only recognisable from each other by different colours of their clothes. How they laughed when sometimes I called one by the wrong name! They were my first best friends in my life and I loved them both.

There was a small farm, about a mile away from us, bordering on the woodland, owned by Kowalski, the middle-aged couple. They kept a few milking cows, some chickens and grew potatoes and other vegetables on their land. My mother and I with my two friends have often helped Kowalski with their farming tasks (I loved feeding chickens!) in exchange for milk, butter, eggs and vegetables

Germans now occupied the whole Poland. The Nazis started to rule, with the "Gestapo" (their murderous police, hunting Jews and dissidents). As children, we were not - at least initially - aware what it meant. We were just glad that the bombardment has stopped.

One day, Rachel came alone to my house.

"Sara wanted to help Mum in the garden," - she said - "but I want to pick up some wild strawberries in the wood. Will you come with me?" Of course, I did.

The forest was full of delicious, red, juicy strawberries, enough to fill our baskets and our stomachs. We enjoyed the feast, till it started getting dark, the time to return home. We stopped at Kowalski farm to give them some strawberries.

Mr. Kowalski (I've forgotten his first name) has ushered us into the house.

"Sylvia," - he said to me - "you go home to your mother - but it'll be better for Rachel to stay here with us."

"Why?" - I asked.

"Because," - he replied in a shaking voice - "I have to tell you the truth. While you were in the wood, the Gestapo took all Jewish people from the town and drove them away somewhere... we don't know where. In this farm we have a place where no one would suspect someone to hide there. Rachel, you can be saved."

Rachel started to cry uncontrollably. Mrs. Kowalski tried to comfort her in her arms.

Mr. Kowalski now turned to me. "Sylvia," - he

spoke in a very serious tone - "if the Gestapo discovers that Rachel is here... all of us: Rachel, I and my wife will be shot on the spot. Do you understand?"

I nodded.

"Remember: never, never tell anyone what you know. It stands a good chance that the Gestapo in their hurry might have been not aware that Sara had a twin sister. There is a hope for Rachel. The war is not going to last for ever... neither will Hitler's rule. Now, Sylvia, go home! Go home and pray for all of us!"

I ran home, sobbing and spilling some strawberries on my way. My mother's face was tear-stained.

"If people ask you where you've been today," - she said - "tell them that you were picking up wild strawberries in the wood alone. Remember, Sylvia: you were there alone!"

That evening we both prayed, saying rosary to Holy Mary - as we used to pray in our underground shelter during the time of the bombardment.

In those days, the only true (and reliable) news were the news whispered confidentially by word of mouth; they were called "underground news". They used to spread quickly. Soon we knew what has happened to Jewish people from our town.

They were taken to a secluded place in the forest few miles away, made to stand at the edge of the deep trench and shot from behind by the machine-gun. All of them: men, women and children; their dead bodies fell to the bottom of the trench. (Some time later it came to our knowledge that the Nazis - after this initial stage of their ethnic cleansing - built the concentration camps and the gas chambers, as "more efficient" in carrying out their diabolic plan.)

At my age of eight, I could not understand why my best friend, Sara and so many others had to be killed because they were Jews - and my mother could not explain it, either. Now, forty-two years later, I still don't understand.

Later on, in England, my husband Eric (who, as a child has lost both parents during the German bombing raid on London - and only survived thanks to the British government's action of evacuating children from the attacked city to the rural countryside), has asked me about my life in war-torn Poland. I told him of the holocaust and of what had happened to my Jewish friends and many others...

"After what you went through," - Eric remarked - "you must hate Germans!"

"No, I don't." - I replied - "Not every German man or woman is a born Nazi. I've heard of

Germans who - like Polish farmers - risked their lives by helping Jewish people to escape their worst fate. I've also heard of the two German men who after the war, when the full horror of the holocaust became well known, committed suicide. They could not live with the feeling of guilt of what has been done in their names. How can I hate people like them?"

"That's true, Sylvia... that's true. In every country in the world many good, wonderful, even heroic people live. And also few evil ones. The hell breaks out when the evil starts to rule!" - Eric paused for a while, then added: "I think that we are using the wrong word, calling human atrocities "bestialities". No animal on this earth - not even so-called "beasts" in the wild jungle who kill for their food, are capable of being as cruel as some people are. The feelings of the unprovoked hatred and sadism are unknown to animals. Maybe we could learn something from them!"

I agreed with what he has said.

As Mr. Kowalski predicted, the war ended in May, 1945. Rachel could now come out of hiding, after four years of living with her protectors on their farm. Only now, I was allowed to see her secret place where she could flee each time when the two guard dogs, running loose would start barking, announcing someone's presence at the gate. The entrance to this place was a little door in the wine cellar (hidden behind the cleverly arranged wine cases), leading through the tunnel to the small vault under the barn, initially made as the shelter from the bombing raids. The entrance from the barn was also concealed by the haycocks.

Rachel ran to me with her arms wide open when we met first time after our long separation. She has grown up, taller and looking older for her age of fourteen, no longer the girl I remembered: care-free, laughing and singing. She became more mature - and more saddened. I was aware that she knew what had happened to her family. But she couldn't talk about it.
"Sylvia!" - she uttered, in tears - "You are my only friend left!"
"You have more friends, Rachel..."
"Yes, I know. Mrs. and Mr. Kowalski are more than friends to me. They are... like my parents..."
We had to take a long walk around the farm to calm down. Then, Rachel told me that her aunt, her mother's close sister who lived in England wanted her to come and to live with her and her family. Rachel felt undecided, as this would mean to say good-bye to both Kowalski... and me.
I then told her that my mother and I (thanks to the Red Cross, who after the war was reuniting broken families) were soon going to join my father in England. I explained that my father, who during

the war was the officer in Polish army and had fought in the western front, was now unwelcome in his country by the new, Russia-imposed communist regime.

Maybe what I've said has helped Rachel to make up her mind. She went to live with her aunt in England. Few months later, I ran fast to embrace my father, who greeted us at the London airport. And in the next week I also met Rachel in her aunt's house where she lived, about twenty miles from us.

* * * * *

At that moment, I stopped reading Sylvia's memoirs and walked to Leo's studio, where he was painting.

"Leo," - I asked - "what was the name of your grandmother who came from Poland?"

"Her name was Rachel." - Leo replied.

"Can you tell me something what she has told you about her life in Poland during the war?"

"Of course I can. She has told me a lot. The memories of the war and of the holocaust are never forgotten by those who know them from their own, hellish experience. Rachel's family, her both parents and her twin sister Sara have been murdered by the German Gestapo, after the raid on the town where they lived. Miraculously, Rachel survived because at the time of the raid she was picking up wild strawberries in the wood with her Polish friend.

On their return, the friendly farmers took care of Rachel; they had some hiding places on their farm. They risked their lives by doing that... Gestapo would shoot on the spot anyone helping Jews.

After the war, Rachel emigrated to England to live there with her aunt. Later, in England she met her old Polish friend... yes, I remember her name: Sylvia! She also kept a close contact with her god-sent protectors in Poland, the farmers.. what was their names? I forgot!"

"Kowalski?" - I prompted.

"Yes, Kowalski! But... how do you know that?"

I handed Leo the envelope with Sylvia's memoirs. "Read this!" I said.

* * * * *

That day, Leo could not finish painting his new picture, as he had planned.

Chapter 13

THE FOOTPRINTS

"Julia," - Leo asked me in the evening - "do you remember the time when we've first met?"

"I do, Leo. We sat on the bench in the college garden. We started talking about the weather... the easy subject for the first meeting! The day was lovely, the sun shining. The golden daffodils in full bloom, all around us on the lawn..."

"What I've felt then, Julia... how can I explain it? This was more then "love at first sight". It was a feeling of almost a certainty that you and I were already linked together... and now, years later, we know: your grandmother and mine were the very close life-long friends!"

"My natural mother and both grandparents died in the road accident few hours before I was born. I've never seen any of them..." - I reflected.

"My grandmother Rachel," - Leo said - "like her husband, died before her old age, when I was a teenager. I still remember her well. Yes, she told me that she had a close Polish friend, but I never thought of it as of something very important. Neither did I tell you much about her. Life was always so busy... no time to dwell on the tragedies, either ours or those of our ancestors. And now, the echoes from the past are catching up with us!"

Leo paused for a while, then added: "Now, I know why at our first meeting I've felt that you and I were no strangers to each other!"

"Leo... at that time I also felt the same way." - I said.

"That's what we call "precognition," - Leo replied - "though we have no clue what it is and how it works! However, not everything can be explained by it. Not what Sylvia has written about Koteck..."

"About Koteck?" - I asked, feeling rather confused.

"Yes. Oh, Julia... you haven't read it all?"

"No. I've stopped my reading to ask you about your grandmother. I had the feeling that something is there what concerns us..."

"Your feeling was right, Julia. Read the last part of Sylvia's memoirs. You'll find more there, telling us about more connections, more links spanning times and places... like the trail of the footprints, made by the small paws of the kitten... of our Koteck!"

With the slightly trembling hand, Leo returned the envelope to me.

* * * * *

It was late - but not too late for me to read the final pages of my granny's memoirs.

Sylvia wrote:

I'll write more about my new life in England: about my nursing job, meeting and marrying Eric, about our dear daughter, Eva. Now I would like to add one more memory from our last days in Poland, before my mother's and my emigration. It is a kind of memory which stays fresh in my mind - and still brings tears to my eyes.

The last week of the February in Poland is usually the time when the first signs of the forthcoming spring begin to appear: snowdrops, making their way through the snow or through the mud; heaps of rapidly thawing snow, sometimes causing flooding. But that year, the last year in my country, the winter returned with a vengeance, with more frost and snowstorms.

Late in the evening, we heard the sound of a plaintive mewing outside. My mother half-opened the door. I looked out from behind her shoulder.

"Oh, it's him, again!" - she exclaimed - " The black kitten that keeps on wandering around! I don't know who is his owner."

"Let him come in, Mum... it is freezing outside!"

"How can we, Sylvia? He has diarrhea, is all dirty! Even if we do, who is going to look after him in few weeks time, when we go to England? It is best for him to go back to his house, where he belongs... now!"

My mother was very strong-willed and I never dared to oppose her openly. I thought I'll wait for the right moment when she will be asleep to open the door. But my mum who knew "my ways" kept the key under her pillow.

The "right moment" came very late, at dawn, when my mother went to the kitchen. I opened the door.

Outside, the black silhouette of the little kitten was still visible under the cover of freshly fallen snow... stiff and cold. My desperate attempts to revive him by cuddling him close, rubbing down his body and praying loud were futile.

My mother touched my shoulder. "It's no use trying, Sylvia..." - she uttered - "it is too late..."

How harsh those two words, "too late" sounded! I restrained myself from shouting at my mum... because her eyes, like mine, were also filled with tears.

It was so hard at night to listen to the kitten's cries for help - and to delay my response... but much harder to listen now to the silence that followed them.

Guilt... gnawing on the bottom of my heart and from time to time - even many years later - breaking out in the most joyful moments in my life... like an intruder, shouting and accusing: "What do you think gives you the right to feel happy? The little creature, crying for help has been denied that right! Other people risked their lives to save one girl... what were your risks? Why you've failed to help?"

I was brought up in the Catholic faith. According to it, every sin could be forgiven by God if one makes confession to the priest, says few prayers and... yes, redresses the wrong done to another, either on the earth or by praying for the departed soul. In my case, the one who has suffered was no longer on this earth and... he had no soul! I was taught by the Church that only humans, and not animals were endowed with the immortal souls.

What I badly needed was not so much the forgiveness for my sin, but rather a hope... even a glimmer of hope to reach my kitten, to take him in my arms, to make him feel loved and cared for... to make him happy!

I badly needed another faith. And another world.

Eric is the amateur astronomer who loves to talk about the galaxies, the universe and the universes, about the "reversible flow of time", et cetera... but I've never fully grasped the subject. Yet, nothing would stop me from day-dreaming of a "place" where I could find shelter and response to my longings... wherever it may be, in any universe!

Guilt... it also made its way into my dreams at night. In those dreams I often found myself in the middle of a vast, snow-bound field, stretching to the horizon on all sides. Nothing there but snow... far and wide, white and bright, here and there glimmering in the last rays of the setting sun. I was looking for my lost kitten and calling him.

He appeared, some distance away: mewing, wading through the snow that was too deep for his tiny paws. I started moving towards him... very slowly, because my feet felt heavy, as if something were pulling them down. When I came closer, few steps only from reaching the kitten, my legs refused to move.

More snow cascaded from the dark cloud above. It was the avalanche. The kitten was no longer visible under the thick, white blanket that also covered me up to my knees - but I still kept at calling, calling him... till the moment when Eric woke me up one night.

"Sylvia," - he said - "you were shouting in your sleep. You were shouting: "Koteck, Koteck!" What this word means?"

I had to calm down. Then I explained that the Polish word "Kotek" (spelled without letter "c") in English means "kitten". In sleep, my memory recalled my native language from the past. And I told Eric the story of the black kitten (whom now I named simply "Koteck") - and of my guilt.

I was glad that my husband didn't offer me the usual "consolation" by excusing me on the ground of my young age at the time, too immature for making an independent decision. This would lead to nowhere.

"It is not you who is crying, Sylvia." - he said - "It is Koteck who cries in your heart."

"I just want him to be happy..." - I murmured.

"What I want to say," - Eric continued - "may sound to many people as "far-fetched" or "too religious", but I want to say it to you, Sylvia. When we have a deep desire, deep enough to become an urge to do something that seems to be impossible in our "usual" way of thinking - then, we have to reach out beyond the limits and the restrictions of this thinking. After all, the greatest discoveries in the history had been made by "making dreams come true."

There are different ways of looking at what we call "soul". One is to deny its existence or to see it as a by-product of the chemical activities of the brain. Once the biological machine dies, everything dies with it - like the sound of a broken record player. Another way is to see every living being not as a biological machine that may have or produce the soul, but as the one who is the soul that temporarily inhabits and activates the body.

I deeply feel that this view is much closer to the truth - the Truth that may elude the grasp of *our reasoning, but not the grasp of our intuition. Because it has the answers to questions that may seem unanswerable.*

Your Koteck, Sylvia... his cries for help are echoing through time and space and are heard by your compassion, if not by your physical hearing. You respond, it is the two-way communication.

There are signs, not always clearly visible, buried under too much of our materialistic thinking, signs leading us to what we long for... like footprints, left by someone who keeps calling: "I am here!" "

I was grateful to Eric for what he has said.

My dream did return, but it was no longer the same dream. Like before, I was looking at the vast snowscape around me - but unlike before, it was now sparkling in the bright sunlight of the day, no evening shadows there. All was peaceful and calm after the recent snowfall. I was walking - or rather sliding along on the surface of the snow. I felt almost like flying!

The horizon line receded, revealing another view: here, at the end of the field, a big tree grew, with the tips of its lowest boughs dipped into snow.

Footprints appeared in front of me, small footprints on the snow, leading to the tree. I followed them. And I heard a sound coming out from that spot... the sound I could not fail to recognise: the low, almost shy mewing.

"Koteck!" - I shouted out.

He was there, under the snow-covered bough, trying to come out. He looked at me with the expression of joy and relief in his eyes. I embraced him, and then... my hands went through the kitten, as if through the air. I realised that was the way I got through the dense branch of the spruce-fir. I could slip through any solid object and leave no trace. But I couldn't lift Koteck and hold him in my arms!

"Help!" - I cried out in despair.

As if in response, a group of people approached us. I didn't know them, yet I felt they were no strangers to me: two women, one man, a small boy and a yellow dog.

The boy shouted: "He is here!" The young woman lifted the tree's bough and took Koteck in her arms. The dog started licking the kitten. Koteck loved that and purred with delight.

I started telling the girl how grateful I felt to her, to the others and to the dog... but she could not hear me. No one could hear me either, no one could see me. No one was even aware of my presence here. No one... except for Koteck, who looked at me once again, his eyes filled with joy, as if saying: "I am happy now!"

This was what I longed for. My dream came true.

* * * * *

Sylvia's memoirs have ended here. Some weeks later, her earthly life has also ended on the Bristol - London motorway.

The end... like the setting sun that returns after the night... to open yet another day with the sunrise.

Chapter 14

FERN FLOWERS ARE SHY

Sunrise... like the one this morning. The dawn, shrouded in the soft, milky fog. All calm and quiet. Birds still asleep in the trees, waiting for the sun to wake them up to start their daily concert.

They came, the rising sun's rays: at first gently, almost shyly trying to find their way through the misty cloud... and finally absorbing the fog into their brightness. Birds started signing their praise of the day.

The time was too good to stay in bed. Leo and Oliver (with Koteck at the edge of his pillow) were sleeping soundly. I left the note for them on the kitchen table and walked to the field.

At its far side, near the path leading to the woods, a big tree, brought down from the slope by the wind, lay on the ground. Angela was sitting there, absorbed in writing something on her notepad. She didn't see me approaching her from behind.

I stood few steps back, not wanting to interrupt her. When she finished writing, she looked for a long time at the woods, then turned her gaze around.

"Oh, Julia!" - she exclaimed - "You too, could

not sleep in such a lovely morning!"

I sat beside her on the broken tree's trunk. "Can I guess: are you writing a poem?"

"I've just finished it. When I am here, Julia... my memory plays back the scenes from the past, when Lacy was running beside me, jumping and barking with joy... I can almost hear her barks! And I still cry, but... but now, I can catch a glimpse of the light at the end of the dark tunnel. I'll read my poem to you:

A HOPE
There, we will walk on boundless fields
Of Great Eternity...
Is this a dream? Misguided wish?
Or... what it comes to be?

We seek the Truth, we reach to grasp
The rainbow in the sky
That comes and goes and leaves us here
To think, to long... and cry.

Pacing the valley of the tears
Among its stones we find
The gleaming treasures of the Hope
That makes us stop and smile.

And wonder: if they are so real,
Where do they all come from?
From rainbows, dropping from the sky
Or my Eternal Home?

"I love this poem, Angela!" I said - "Yes, it is hope that illuminates and shows us the way out of darkness."

"I had dwelled in this darkness for some time, Julia, in grief that seemed to be hopeless. I know what it is. I know what it feels like falling off a broken bridge. And yet... the flowing current took me to another bridge, stronger... indestructible.

Yes, hope is the way out of darkness. At first, a way to a belief that the one's very dear wish can be fulfilled, but still not feeling quite certain whether it will be or not. And then, something happens. What one longs for, what one searches for suddenly appears and shouts out: "Look, I'm here!" Then, the uncertain belief becomes the certainty. Now, I no longer *believe,* but I *know.*

Julia, once more thanks for letting me read Sylvia's memoirs. It was then when this certainty has dawned on me: there are many dimensions of the great Reality, many universes yet to be discovered. Countless possibilities in the Eternity.

Our Koteck, Julia... or rather" - she smiled - "Sylvia's Kotek, without letter 'c'... once out of his body and its restrictions, how far and fast he could fly, flash, zoom across the universes, through times and spaces... from the snow-bound garden in Poland to the snow-bound field in England, in another time...back to the earth, in his new physical body, so he could be loved here by someone, responding to Sylvia's calls, the calls of her grief and guilt, the calls of her love..."

Angela paused for a while, then added with a smile: "How wonderful is to know that feline souls can jump much higher than over garden fences!"

"As any other soul can?" - I inquired.

"No doubt!" - Angela exclaimed - "Some time ago I read in a book (I forgotten its title!) what one mystic has said. He said: *'Foundation of Universe is Love.'* It follows that everyone, every living being is never deprived of love... not a single sparrow nestling, killed by a predator before it had a chance to spread its wings. Not one child... like Sara, Rachel's twin sister, murdered by evil people.

If Love is the foundation of everything that exists, there is no place it cannot reach. The Eternity is populated with souls... and with the angelic beings who care and who respond. No one is ever abandoned. No one forgotten. When Love motivates the desire, the possibilities become endless."

* * * * *

She was silent for some time, her gaze fixed on the path, leading up to the wood.

"Oh, look!" - she suddenly cried out excitedly. On the bottom of the path, only few yards away, a fox stood, watching us.

"He looks like the one..." - I wondered - "that I, Leo and Lacy met in this wood eight or nine years ago. I've told you about it: Lacy wanted to play with him, but the fox was too shy to play with a dog!"

"It could be the same one," - Angela laughed - "or another, a younger one. If he is the same fox, who knows? It could be that he has changed his mind and decided to play now, but..." - the smile has suddenly gone from her face - "there is no dog around he can see and play with..."

The fox was still observing us curiously for a minute or two, then - just as it happened before - he turned back and disappeared in the bushes.

* * * * *

The sun was now rising higher and higher into the sky. The yellow dandelions around us, at this time of the year dominating the meadows, sparkled in its light and looked more golden than yellow. The time came to return home.

"Sometimes, when I walk here on this path," - Angela reflected - "my mind recalls the time when we were returning home from the wood, on the night of the summer solstice, in the moonlight. I felt so happy, so exalted by what I've seen there! And then, a sad thought has crossed my mind: "why *only* me?" And I felt lonely..."

"Because, Angela," - I replied - "at that time you were only five. Your heart and your mind were fresh and open, full of trust... not yet burdened with what life and the society throws at us."

"Yes, I know it now. I also know that what has unfolded itself before our eyes: the story created by the calls of despair, guilt, longing and love... the tale all alive, echoing throughout the universes and all the way marking its paths with the little kitten's footprints... is not unique! Our family is not exceptional. So-called 'strange coincidences' or 'miracles' do happen more often than they are reported. People don't talk about them for fear of being ridiculed. The fear of becoming an outcast is quite powerful."

"Also," I added - "there are others who are impatient. They are explorers. Like someone who may one day wade through a shallow tide on a beach, scoop some sea water into his cup, examine it and proclaim that now he knows *everything* about the vast, deep and unfathomable ocean. Someone else does likewise - but his water sample, collected in another place and time, is not the same.

The two collectors start arguing which cup contains the Truth and which one doesn't. Then they start fighting. Their followers start wars. The history of humanity is heavy with the burden of atrocities, committed in names of different gods. Who could see the celestial flowers through this thick, murky fog, hanging over the earth?"

"Or, maybe..." - Angela wondered - "those gifts, sent to us from the celestial realm, would love to fill the places they find lacking in flowers. Maybe on the night of the summer solstice they hover over the ferns... the ferns, primordial ferns, for millions of years surviving all twists and jerks of evolution, yet failing to bloom... maybe the heavenly flowers are eager to land there, but they are scared away by this murky fog of our thoughts and deeds... *fern flowers are shy!*"

THE END